## Don't Walk This Way

"Wait," Bess called out excitedly. "Don't forget your shoes."

Bess hurried over to the shoes near the clothing rack, and as she carried them to Miss Zaza, I noticed two wet footprints on the floor—wet spots left by the shoes!

I started to panic as I did the math: Wet shoes . . . plus electric costume . . . equals disaster!

"Stop—Zaza, stop!" I shouted. "Don't dare step into those shoes!"

# NANCY DREW

**Available from Aladdin**

CAROLYN KEENE

# NANCY DREW

*GIRL DETECTIVE®*

**#46**

## Mystery at Malachite Mansion

Book Two in the
Malibu Mayhem Trilogy

Aladdin
New York   London   Toronto   Sydney   New Delhi

This book is a work of fiction. Any references to historical events, real people, or real locales are used fictitiously. Other names, characters, places, and incidents are the product of the author's imagination, and any resemblance to actual events or locales or persons, living or dead, is entirely coincidental.

☙ALADDIN
An imprint of Simon & Schuster Children's Publishing Division
1230 Avenue of the Americas, New York, NY 10020
First Aladdin paperback edition October 2011
Copyright © 2011 by Simon & Schuster, Inc.
All rights reserved, including the right of reproduction in whole
or in part in any form.
ALADDIN is a trademark of Simon & Schuster, Inc., and related logo is a registered trademark of Simon & Schuster, Inc.
NANCY DREW, NANCY DREW: GIRL DETECTIVE, and
related logo are registered trademarks of Simon & Schuster, Inc.
For information about special discounts for bulk purchases, please contact
Simon & Schuster Special Sales at 1-866-506-1949 or business@simonandschuster.com.
The Simon & Schuster Speakers Bureau can bring authors to your live event.
For more information or to book an event, contact the Simon & Schuster Speakers
Bureau at 1-866-248-3049 or visit our website at www.simonspeakers.com.
Designed by Karina Granda
The text of this book was set in Bembo.
Manufactured in the United States of America 0911 OFF
10 9 8 7 6 5 4 3 2 1
Library of Congress Control Number 2011934220
ISBN 978-1-4424-2297-1 (pbk)
ISBN 978-1-4424-2298-8 (eBook)

# Contents

# SABOTAGED SEA

"**M**y beach!" Stacey Manning cried. "My beautiful white sandy beach!"

Bess, George, and I didn't know what to say.

We wished we could console Stacey as she watched clumps of oil wash up on her private beach, but we felt just as badly as she did.

It was "the morning after." Just yesterday afternoon, a luxurious yacht had exploded off the coast, sending gallons of oil spilling onto the shores of Malibu's rich and trendy Malachite Beach. Stacey, a celebrity event planner, had just returned from Las Vegas to check out the damage. The blackened sands and oil-slicked dune grass wasn't much of a welcome, to say the least.

"No matter how I try, I can't understand it," Stacey said. "How can one burning yacht create such a major spill?" She held her nose to block out the acrid smell in the air.

"The yacht was carrying drums of diesel oil," I explained. "When Bess and I were on the cruise, we found the drums underneath a tarp. Add the oil to the yacht's own tank and *kaboom!*"

"You mean the *cult* cruise," Bess said with a frown.

"Cult cruise" was right. I still couldn't believe Bess and I had gone undercover to investigate a brainwashing cult being run right next door to Stacey's beach house. Our vacation in Malachite had started out so perfectly. Stacey had invited the three of us—me and my best friends Bess Marvin and George Fayne—to spend a few weeks at her house while she worked an event in Las Vegas. Stacey had once worked with George's mom, but Mrs. Fayne had lost touch with her over the years, until Stacey called out of the blue with her awesome invite to California.

At first we thought the beachfront mansion at the secluded end of the beach was some kind of trendy spa, but we soon found out the truth: Roland's Renewal Retreat and Spa was a front for a brainwashing, money-stealing cult.

Stacey pulled out her smartphone to check for texts.

"Just when you think you know your neighbors," Stacey said with a sigh, her eyes still on her phone. "Roland's Retreat opened up less than a year ago. I hardly knew him and certainly didn't know he was running a crazy New Age cult."

"Bess and I found out firsthand," I said, shuddering at the memory. "Roland made his followers walk across hot coals, verbally abuse one another, and meditate inside a tent that had to be over a hundred degrees."

"Until we passed out," Bess added. "Roland called it a sweat lodge."

"You mean a *death* lodge," George said. "If I hadn't heard screams coming from the tent, I never would have called the police, and you guys would have been . . . I don't even want to say it."

Stacey gazed out at the smoldering yacht on the ocean. "The most important thing is that you were rescued, even if Roland did manage to take revenge."

I watched as black oil washed up on the beach. After Bess, George, and I had blown the whistle on Roland, he refused to be taken alive. Before the police could come arrest him, he blew up his yacht— and himself. It was Roland's way of going out in a blaze of glory. He got the blaze part—although I saw no glory in destroying a beach and its wildlife.

"Such a tragedy," Stacey said, and sighed again. "No one will want to build or buy property on Malachite Beach now."

She turned to us and said, "By the way . . . whatever happened to Roland's second-in-command, Inge?"

"You mean his sidekick?" I asked. "Inge was taken in by the police yesterday. We saw it ourselves."

Stacey stole another look at her phone before saying, "I never did like that silly woman. And to think she was once nominated for an Academy Award."

I was surprised Stacey knew so much about the tall blond woman with the frosty voice—especially after admitting that she hardly knew her neighbors. But this was Hollywood, the land of celebrity gossip, where everyone knew everyone else's business.

"An Academy Award?" Bess said, her blue eyes flashing. "Was Inge an actress?"

"A makeup artist," Stacey said. "She worked on those low-budget horror movies. I think her biggest one was called *Zombie Nightmare at Camp Telluride*."

I smiled. "Camp *Terrified*. We saw it a few Halloweens ago."

"That creepy Eddy Fluegel with the worms crawling out of his ears gave me serious goose bumps," Bess said, pretending to shiver.

"And you gave me scratches and scabs," George said. "You dug your nails into my arm throughout the whole movie, Bess."

I smiled at my two best friends. It was hard for anyone—even me sometimes—to believe they were cousins. George, with her dark hair and eyes, was a computer geek, and when it came to her clothes, comfort was essential. Bess's closet was stuffed with clothes that never got dirty—even when she repaired cars or whatever else needed fixing. Unfortunately, Bess couldn't fix Malachite Beach, and I wondered if anyone could. The coast guard was still working at extinguishing the last of the yacht's burning debris.

"You know what's even scarier than Eddy Fluegel?" Bess asked, nodding at the ocean. "The thought of Roland washing up onto the beach."

"You mean his corpse?" I asked.

"She means don't even go there," George said. "Bess, Roland—or Marty Malone—is probably shark chow by now."

"Did you say Marty Malone?" Stacey asked.

"That was Roland's real name," I explained. "We found out during our investigation. We also discovered his true occupation: career criminal."

"I'm sorry those degenerates had to spoil your vacation," Stacey said, again glancing down at her phone. "Let me just enter something into my schedule . . . eleven a.m., book return flights for girls . . ."

Bess, George, and I traded confused looks. *Return* flights?

"We're not going back to River Heights," George told Stacey.

Stacey looked up. "You're not?" she asked.

I shook my head, though I had to admit River Heights was looking pretty good right now—especially after what we'd been through. I missed my boyfriend, Ned, and my dad with his lawyerly advice. And I totally craved our housekeeper Hannah Gruen's comfort food and hugs, but my friends and I still had work to do—and this time it wasn't detective work.

"We've decided to stick around and help clean up the beach, Stacey," I said.

"Clean up the beach?" Stacey repeated slowly.

"We still have more than two weeks to go on our vacation. We might as well do something useful," George said.

Stacey stared at us silently. "You'll be wasting your time. There's no way anyone can clean up this disaster in two weeks—"

"Stacey!" a voice shouted.

Stacey frowned at the interruption. I did too when I saw who it was—the famous Casabian sisters walking over from their own private beach.

Not that I wasn't happy to see the über-glam Mandy and Mallory. We had become friends with the sisters when we tried to rescue their younger sister, Mia, from Roland's cult. What I *wasn't* happy to see was the producer and camera crew from their reality show, *Chillin' with the Casabians*.

Hurrying to catch up with them was Mia. She had been totally brainwashed in Roland's cult, but the glazed zombie look in her eyes seemed to be gone.

"Okay, everybody!" Bev, the producer, shouted. "Group hug for the camera. Group hug!"

Stacey seemed to grit her teeth as Mandy and Mallory wrapped their arms around her.

"Oh, Stacey, isn't it just horrible?" Mallory cried, flipping her long dark hair over her shoulder. "Our beach on Villa Fabuloso is a gross mess too!"

Bev stared at Mandy as she pointed to the camera.

"Oh, yeah," Mandy blurted as she seemed to remember. She looked directly into the camera and quickly added, "But wait until you hear our big news!"

"What is it?" Stacey sighed.

"We've called a meeting of our Malachite neighbors at two thirty this afternoon," Mandy explained. "To talk about the oil slick and what we can do to help."

"Will it be on your reality show?" I said, hoping not.

"Isn't everything?" Bev asked.

"Here's the fun part," Mallory said, smiling at us. "You guys are invited to the meeting too."

"Seriously?" Bess gasped.

"Sure," Mallory replied. "You're our neighbors, even if it's just temporary."

Bess squeezed my arm in excitement. A meeting of Malachite residents meant *celebrities*!

The three of us were totally amped, but when I looked over at Stacey, her mouth hung open in astonishment.

"A meeting to save the beach?" she asked incredulously.

"That's right," Mandy said. "We thought you'd be pleased, Stacey."

The camera was on Stacey as she shook her head. "People on Malachite don't do a thing for themselves," she said. "Do you really expect them to pick up clumps of oil and dead fish?"

I couldn't understand why Stacey wasn't more supportive or even excited about the party. Didn't she want to save her own beach and property?

"I think it's a brilliant idea," I told the Casabian sisters. "You never know what people are willing to do— even those from Malachite—unless you ask them."

"If you ask me, we're wasting our time," Stacey said as she entered the meeting into her phone. "But I'll be there."

Without saying good-bye, she walked toward her house. She didn't realize that Bev and the camera crew were trailing her halfway up the beach.

"Somebody didn't have her coffee this morning," Mandy said when Stacey left.

"Right?" Mallory agreed. "What's up with her?"

"Come on, give Stacey some slack," George said. "She's seriously upset about her beach. I'd be too if our river at home looked like the inside of a sewer."

Bev hurried back with the crew. She motioned to Mallory and whispered, "Bring up the doctor . . . the doctor."

"Oh—yeah!" Mallory said. She threw back her shoulders. "I am happy to announce that I have an appointment with Dr. Raymond today—he's a world-famous Beverly Hills plastic surgeon."

"Plastic surgeon?" George groaned. She looked the sisters up and down. "You're kidding, right?"

"Never! It'll probably be a little nip here, a tuck there. You know—that kind of stuff," Mallory answered.

I rolled my eyes. Mallory was fine just the way she was—but this was Hollywood, where fine never seemed to be good enough.

"Dr. Raymond has his own reality show too," Mandy went on. "So our reality show will be on his reality show."

"And vice versa," Mallory added.

"Cut!" Bev shouted practically in my ear. "I have the shots I need. Let's go back to Villa Fabuloso and talk about the next scene."

"Good riddance," George said under her breath.

I was happy the crew was leaving. They were like an annoying mosquito you couldn't swat.

Mandy and Mallory followed Bev and the crew back to their own beach house. Mia lagged behind to stare at the oily crud scattered on the beach. She had been so quiet all this time that I'd almost forgotten she was there.

"How do you feel, Mia?" I asked.

Mia had been severely dehydrated after Roland's sweat lodge, just like Bess and I had been.

"Much better." Mia smiled at us. "That brainwashing serum they injected me with is finally leaving my system."

"We can tell," Bess said cheerily. "You're no longer talking like a—"

"Like a robot?" Mia cut in with a laugh. "That must have been pretty freaky."

"You couldn't help it," I said. "Luckily, you'll never have to worry about Roland again. The coast guard can't find a trace of him after the explosion."

"As Roland said himself," George said with a smirk, "garbage in, garbage out."

I cringed as George repeated the words Roland's followers had chanted as they prepared to dump garbage from his yacht into the ocean. According to Roland, the trash-dump exercise reflected the release of negative thoughts. Not only had Roland messed with people's minds, he'd also messed up the ocean. In fact, our whole investigation had started when George accidentally stepped on a washed-up hypodermic needle.

"Thanks for helping me, you guys," Mia said. "And everybody else in that crazy cult."

As Mia made her way to Villa Fabuloso, I heard a familiar *chop-chop-chop* noise. I looked up and saw several helicopters hovering overhead.

"Probably news crews," I decided.

"They should get a shot of that." Bess pointed to the dead fish on the beach. "I have a feeling this is just the beginning."

Bess and I were about to decide what to do with the poor fish when I heard George shout, "Whoa!"

"More dead fish?" I asked.

"More dead *something*," George replied.

She wasn't kidding: Washing up onto the beach was . . . a coffin!

# GREEN . . . OR MEAN

**M**y stomach plunged. I tried to stay calm as waves crashed against the long rectangular box.

"Maybe it's not what we think it is," I said.

"With the words 'Rest in Peace' on the lid?" Bess said. "I'll take a wild guess and say it's a coffin."

The three of us waded slowly toward the coffin, stopping about two feet away from it, staring silently.

"Who do you think is inside?" I finally asked.

"I don't know . . . Roland?" Bess said.

"How would Roland get his dead hands on a coffin?" George snorted.

I was about to grab my phone to call the police when I noticed other letters scrawled across the lid. Underneath REST IN PEACE were the words MALACHITE BEACH.

"'Rest in peace, Malachite Beach'? What does that mean?" I asked, just as a strong wave crashed onto the beach. It knocked the coffin on its side, popping the lid open.

Bess shrieked and turned to run. So did I until George grabbed my arm.

"Wait! Wait, you guys!" George cried. "It's empty!"

Bess and I froze in our tracks. Turning back toward the coffin, I saw George was right. Nobody was inside. In fact, *nothing* was inside.

"Snap!" a voice said, and laughed. "We punked them good!"

About ten yards away on the water was a motorboat. Four people dressed in bright blue wet suits rocked the boat as they high-fived one another. They looked like they were in their late teens or maybe early twenties.

"Did they say we were punked?" George asked.

I nodded. "They must know something about that stupid coffin."

The boat drifted toward shore before we could ask. Two of the passengers, a guy and a girl, jumped out. Their flippers splashed through shallow water before they stepped onto the beach.

"Hey!" the girl greeted us. She glanced at the empty coffin and smiled. "Thanks for coming to the funeral."

The guy laughed. "Oh, man. You should have seen your faces when that lid popped open. Too funny!"

*Not!* I thought. Who were these people in blue? And what was the deal with the message on the lid? First, an introduction was in order.

"I'm Nancy," I said, forcing a smile. "These are my friends Bess and George."

"George?" The girl looked straight at George. "Your real name must be Georgina, right?"

"Georgina?" George said disdainfully.

"Or Georgette," the guy weighed in. "Yeah, I'll bet it's Georgette."

George's face burned bright red before she snapped, "It's Georgia, all right? Georgia like the state!"

"Okay, okay," the guy said, holding up both hands. "Don't bite my head off!"

I was surprised. George never admitted to her real name—she must really hate the names Georgina and Georgette.

"Now that you know who *we* are, who are you?" I asked.

"Cassie," the girl answered.

"Nathan," the guy said. He nodded to the boat. "And those goofs over there need no introduction."

"Heard that, loser!" one of them shouted back.

George turned to Cassie and Nathan. She pointed at the beached coffin and said, "Speaking of goofs, that was a lame joke you played on us."

"It wasn't meant to be a joke," Cassie said.

"Your *reaction* was what made it funny," Nathan declared.

"Well, it wasn't funny for us," Bess admitted.

"Whatever," Cassie said. Her eyes narrowed as she gazed at the mansions along the beach. "Will you check out the McMansions around here? Total waste of good beach."

"Not to mention a waste of power to light and heat those monstrosities," Nathan said angrily.

"That one over there," Cassie said, pointing to Stacey's house. "Is it yours?"

"It belongs to a friend," I said. "We're staying with her a few extra days to help clean up the beach."

"A few days? Hey, don't knock yourselves out," Cassie said sarcastically.

"*Our* mission to save the beach is a lifelong commitment," Nathan said.

"Mission?" I repeated.

"Sure," Cassie said. "Haven't you heard of the Blue Greenies?"

"Blue Greenies?" Bess giggled. "Sounds like a Pee Wee softball team."

Cassie glared at Bess as if to say, *Don't even go there*.

"The Blue Greenies are a California-based environmental group," Nathan stated. "Dedicated to protecting the ocean and its beaches."

"If you're all about saving the beach," I said with a smile, "then you're in the right place."

George wasn't smiling; her eyes burned at Cassie and Nathan. "I've heard of your troublemaking group," she said. "You use scare tactics to get your messages across. Like that coffin you sent us."

"So it freaked you out a little," Cassie said. "No big deal."

"So what about all those *McMansions* you set on fire?" George asked. "I heard all about that, too."

Fires? I stared at the Blue Greenies. That was a lot more serious than a prank.

"Don't believe everything you hear," Nathan sneered.

"Right now our goal is to spread awareness of the damage done to the beach," Cassie said.

"While protecting our beaches and waters from oppressive members of the human race," Nathan added.

"Only one human was responsible for the disaster on this beach," I said. "One *crazy* human named Roland."

"If you want to help clean the beach," George told

Cassie and Nathan, "why don't you start by picking up that coffin?"

We watched while they hoisted the coffin and carried it through the shallow water to the boat. Their friends pulled it onto the boat, and then Cassie and Nathan climbed in.

"See you!" Cassie called as the boat zoomed off.

"I'm not sure I *want* to see them again," Bess said over the roar of the motor.

"If they were so committed to cleaning up the beach, they would have offered to help us pick up oil clumps," George said. "Or scrub down some stained dune grass."

"They're too busy thinking up ridiculous pranks," I said. "Who needs them anyway? Let's grab those gloves Stacey keeps in her shed and start ourselves."

The three of us sidestepped the washed-up debris until we reached the shed near Stacey's house. Once inside I spotted Stacey's black wet suit, hanging from a hook. I was about to walk past it when I noticed water on the floor right below it.

"That's strange—it looks like there's a puddle under the suit," I said. Then I touched it. It was wet all right.

"Maybe Stacey went for a dive after she got back to Malachite this morning," George suggested.

"She just got back a couple of hours ago," I said.

"She wouldn't have had enough time to go swimming."

"Who in their right mind would go swimming in that ocean now?" Bess asked. "Thanks to Roland, it's totally gross."

"Girls," Stacey's voice called from outside. "George, Bess, Nancy!"

I let go of the suit and answered, "Coming!"

"Wait," George whispered to us. "Not a word about the diving suit, okay?"

"Okay," I said, but really didn't understand why.

As we left the shed we saw Stacey on her deck, pacing back and forth.

"There you are!" she said, waving to us with her smartphone. "Where have you been?"

"We were looking for work gloves so we could clean up the beach," I said.

Stacey leaned over the railing. "Well, forget about that, at least for now," she said. "The meeting of the Malachite minds begins in about an hour."

"At your house?" I asked.

"Here?" Stacey said with a snort. "Actually, I got a call that Don Salazar had offered his beach house for the meeting. Have you heard of him?"

Bess squealed, making me jump. "Are you kidding me? Don Salazar is just about the hottest director in Hollywood and the world!"

"The king of romantic comedies," I added.

Stacey nodded and said, "I planned the premiere party for his latest movie, *Dionysus and Me*. I had Don and his wife enter in a horse-drawn chariot. The press ate it up."

"When are we leaving?" Bess asked excitedly.

Stacey answered by entering the time on her phone and saying out loud, "Meet on deck at one thirty p.m. At one thirty-five, walk down beach to Don's mansion."

With Stacey preoccupied with her phone, I asked George, "Okay, so why didn't you want us to mention the diving suit?"

"Because we're still Stacey's guests," George said. "The last thing I want her to think is that we were snooping around."

"We're detectives," Bess teased. "Snooping is what we do best."

We climbed the steps to the deck and entered the house. I couldn't wait to go to the meeting and possibly meet some of my favorite celebs, but I couldn't stop wondering about the damp diving suit—and the puddle on the floor.

*Someone used Stacey's diving suit and not long ago,* I thought as I followed my friends into the house. *If it wasn't Stacey, then who?*

## CELEBRITY SQUABBLE

"**W**elcome, everybody, welcome!" Mallory declared. "I am, like, so totally psyched that you could all make it."

"Who would miss this?" Bess whispered to me, secretly snapping pictures of everyone with her phone.

"Take a few minutes to say hi to each other," Mandy piped up. "Then we'll start the meeting."

I was pretty excited myself. I looked up and down the long polished mahogany table. It seemed everybody in Don Salazar's palatial dining room was somebody noteworthy—a famous actress, fashion designer, baseball player, comedian—and of course super-famous director Don Salazar himself. The Casabian sisters' camera crew and producer were no-shows, which was fine with me.

While everyone traded greetings around the table, I noticed a girl of about twelve sitting across from Bess, George, and me. She opened a notebook and uncapped a pen. Was she an actress? A singer?

The girl must have felt me staring at her. She looked up, smiled, and said, "Hi."

"Oh, hi," I said. "I'm Nancy. These are my friends Bess and George. We're Stacey Manning's guests for a few weeks."

"Alice Bothwell," the girl said, not shyly. "I live here in Malachite with my family."

"Let me guess," George said. "You're a celebrity too?"

"Not yet," Alice said with a laugh. "Someday I'd like to be the mayor of Malachite Beach, but first we have to clean up the place, right?"

"Right!" I said with a grin. Not only did Alice have a big dream, but she would also be a big help.

Alice suddenly leaned over the table and whispered, "Truth: Cleaning up the beach is the main reason I'm here . . . but not the only reason."

"What's the other reason?" Bess whispered back.

Alice's eyes darted to the left. "He's sitting three chairs down," she said. "But don't make it look obvious!"

We followed Alice's gaze to see a cute teenage guy with sandy brown hair reaching out to grab some cheese on a cracker. I knew who he was immediately.

"Hey, that's Austin Gruber, the singer," I whispered. "What's he doing here?"

"Austin lives on Malachite Beach with his mom and sister," Alice said, her voice still low. "When I found out he was volunteering to help the beach, I thought it was so cool."

"My sister Maggie's also an extreme fan," Bess said. "She even named her gerbil Austin."

Austin leaned back in his chair, but his eyes were no longer on the grapes or the cheese platter.

"Hey, Bess," George teased. "Don't look now, but Austin Gruber is checking you out."

"Stop," Bess said. But she glanced over at him anyway. As their eyes met, they both blushed.

Bess Marvin had practically written the book on flirtation, so it was funny to see her act shy, but no guy had ever been Austin Gruber!

"Meeting's starting," Alice said excitedly as Mandy tapped a glass for attention. As organizers of the meeting, the Casabians sat at the head of the table. "Next we'd like to thank Don for the use of his house," Mandy said with a nod to the director. "Thank you, Don!"

"No problem!" Don boomed. He gestured to the overflowing cheese and fruit platters on the table. "Please, help yourselves. The Scandinavian moose cheese is excellent."

"Did he say *moose* cheese?" I whispered.

"I'll stick to the cheddar," Bess whispered back.

The meeting was turned over to a silver-haired actress named Joanne Stonestreet.

"Okay, everybody," Joanne said. "We're all here for the same reason. Our beloved beaches have been damaged by an unfortunate environmental disaster."

"Tell me about it," said another Malachite resident. "Dead fish covered my beach."

"The smell is unbearable," a nighttime talk show host added. "It's making my son's asthma worse."

"Not to mention what this will do to the value of our houses," Don said. "Leonard Stamp will never build those mansions he was planning on Malachite Beach."

"Well, then," Stacey said with a half smile. "Mr. Stamp will just have to build elsewhere."

The name Leonard Stamp definitely rang a bell. He was a real-estate mogul, a celebrity in his own right. I wasn't surprised he had plans to build on Malachite, one of the trendiest and wealthiest areas in the United States.

"What we need to do is move forward to rescue our beach and the wildlife," said Mia.

"Yes, but it'll take tons of money to clean up the beach, people," Stacey said. "We'll need booms, skimmers—"

"We're rich," Mallory said, tossing her hair. "Like . . . aren't we?"

"Not that rich," Stacey said. "Since this is a man-made disaster, we're not eligible for government support."

All eyes turned to Stacey. She was still skeptical about saving the beach, although I had to admit she seemed to know what she was talking about.

"Well, then," Don said. "We'll have to find a way to raise money."

"How?" Mandy asked.

A bunch of ideas were thrown out—a fashion show, a telethon, an auction—until Alice's hand shot up in the air. "How about a party?" she said.

"A party?" Stacey repeated.

"This year in school we had a party in the gym to raise money for new computers," Alice said. "Everyone who came made a donation. Not only did we get some really cool computers for the school," she continued, "we had enough money left over for a frozen yogurt machine in the cafeteria!"

"Come to think of it," I said, "we did something similar in our high school when we were juniors."

"Except we raised money to buy new sports equipment," George said.

"This isn't middle or high school, girls," Stacey said frostily. "And it certainly isn't River Heights."

"Exactly," I said. "This is Hollywood, so you can invite A-list celebrities and entertainment executives. I think Alice has a great idea." And I reached across the table to give her a high five.

Don smiled and said, "I like it. I think I like it."

"So do Mallory, Mia, and I," Mandy said excitedly.

"Excuse me, excuse me," said Stacey, practically standing up. "Speaking as an event planner—do you have any clue what goes into putting together a party of this magnitude?"

"No, but you do," Don said. "Which is why we need you."

"Absolutely, Stacey," Joanne agreed. "When it comes to event planning, you're the best. We'll need top-notch entertainment, gourmet food, and great guests, so only the best event planner will do."

Stacey's eyes lit up at the word "best." I had a funny feeling Joanne had just said the magic word.

"Well," Stacey said, a smile coming slowly to her face, "I suppose I could throw in my two cents."

Mallory popped up from her chair. She held up her hand and said, "All those in favor of having a fabulous party to raise money to save the beach say aye!"

"Aye!" everyone around the table declared.

"Ye-es!" Alice cheered, pumping her fist. Her idea to have a party to save the beach was official.

"Now," Stacey said, "before I get to work, I'll need to set up some kind of headquarters for the event. You know, a place where the entertainment can rehearse, where we can have meetings—"

"What about your house, Stacey?" Bess asked.

"My place is a dollhouse compared to the rest of the mansions," Stacey said. "Before the oil slick, Leonard Stamp had plans to tear it down."

Bess, George, and I traded surprised looks. That was news to us.

"We'd offer Villa Fabuloso," Mandy said. "But our camera crew is there practically every day."

When no one else volunteered, Stacey shrugged. "I think we should use Roland's house, next door to mine."

"The mansion?" Bess gasped.

I couldn't believe it either. Roland's Renewal Retreat and Spa was where his evil escapades had begun.

Cynthia Wall, a high-profile lawyer, shook her head. "No can do, Stacey," she said. "If Roland is dead, his will has to go through probate. His mansion may have to go to his estate."

"Not if it was rented," Stacey said.

"Rented?" said Cynthia.

"I happen to know that Roland didn't own the mansion," Stacey explained. "It was a rental."

How did Stacey know *that*? She must have been a nosier neighbor than I thought.

"Stacey is right," a red-haired woman piped up. "Roland was renting it from our real-estate agency."

"I say we pay the rent on Roland's mansion for a month," Stacey suggested. "That will give us plenty of time to use the house as our headquarters. We can even use the beach for the event."

"The rent can't be cheap," Don said.

"It's a small price to pay for the donations we'll get for saving the beach," Stacey pointed out.

We thought we had seen the last of that horrible mansion at the end of the beach—and its horrible memories.

"I might be able to persuade a certain celebrity chef to provide the food," Stacey said, working her smartphone. "And since a party isn't a party without great entertainment, I'll see who's available—"

"Um . . . Stacey?" Austin cut in, raising his hand as if he was in school.

Stacey looked up from her phone "What?" she asked.

"I can sing at the party," Austin said.

"That would be epic!" Alice said excitedly. "You have a new CD coming out, right, Austin?"

"Yeah. Actually," Austin said with a smile to Alice, "I wrote four of the songs myself."

"Kids, kids, this isn't a scout jamboree," Stacey cut in. "We need a more grown-up act."

"But—," Austin started to say, but then Mandy interrupted.

"I can get"—she paused for effect—"Miss Zaza to sing at the party."

All heads turned her way, and for good reason. Miss Zaza was the hottest performer around. She was famous for her powerful voice and her outrageous costumes, which she designed herself.

"You *know* Miss Zaza?" Bess asked.

"Sure," Mandy said. "Mallory and I hang with Zaza every now and then."

Mallory nodded as if it was no big deal. But Bess, George, and I were awed.

"If Miss Zaza is at the party," I said, "think of the donations it'll bring in."

"Miss Zaza would be ideal!" Stacey said. "Now *that's* the kind of entertainment I'm talking about."

Alice cleared her throat. She nodded her head in the direction of Austin as if to say, *Remember him?*

*Oops.* I glanced at Austin sinking into his chair, his eyes cast downward.

"I forgot about Austin," I whispered to Bess and George. "Poor guy."

"People—I have another idea," Stacey announced. "Since we're cleaning up the ocean and the beach, let's make this event about conserving *and* celebrating sea life. Zaza can dress up like some glam octopus or something."

"Zaza once rocked a dress made out of cooked lobsters," Mallory said. "She wore it to the Grammy Awards this year."

"I am sure she'll think of something," Stacey said. "I'd also like to fill the swimming pool at the mansion with actual sea creatures."

"What kind of sea life were you thinking about, Stacey?" Mia asked. "Turtles . . . exotic tropical fish?"

"You'll see. I may be full of ideas—but I'm also full of surprises," she said.

Stacey then turned to another woman at the table. "Luellen, you're a publicist. I want tons of publicity on this event."

"You got it, Stace," Luellen said with a nod. "I'll arrange a press conference for later today."

"And my name is spelled with an *e*," Stacey added. "You wouldn't believe how many publicists have left out the *e*. It's so unprofessional."

After watching Stacey closely, I whispered to Bess and George, "I can't believe it. Just minutes ago Stacey was trashing the idea of saving the beach. Now she couldn't be more into it."

"Flattery must go a long way in this town," George whispered back.

The "rich and famous" had to hurry back to movie sets, fashion studios, and tennis lessons, so after Mandy thanked everyone, the meeting was adjourned.

"We'll be getting in touch as the plans proceed," Stacey said, blowing kisses at everyone as they left. "Luellen, wait for me," she called, and ran to catch up with the publicist. Alice came over to say good-bye too.

"Congratulations on having the winning idea, Alice," I said.

"Whatever I can do to help," Alice said. She then handed me a page from her pad with a number scribbled on it. "And in case you guys ever need to know anything about Malachite or its neighbors— just text me."

"Thanks, Alice," I said, taking the number.

"Wow," said George as Alice walked away. "For a twelve-year-old, that kid is no slouch."

"Maybe she *will* be mayor of Malachite Beach someday," Bess said.

Bess, George, and I were thrilled when Don

Salazar himself walked us to the door. "So how do you girls know Stacey?" he asked.

"My mom is an event planner too," George explained. "She worked with Stacey on a few events years ago. They lost touch until Stacey called my mom to lend us her beach house for a few weeks."

Don smiled, shook his head, and said, "That Stacey—so unpredictable."

"You heard what she said," I said. "She's full of ideas *and* surprises."

Once outside, we walked across the beaches back to Stacey's house. It seemed as though oil and debris were everywhere we stepped.

"Can you believe Don Salazar spoke to us?" Bess said, practically skipping along the sand. "To think we'll be seeing all those celebrities and more at the party."

"We might even see them *before* the party," I said. "Maybe Stacey will ask us to help out at her headquarters."

Bess stopped short. "I hope not, Nancy," she said. "Headquarters means Roland's old mansion. No way do I want to spend time there."

Neither did I. Being locked in an out-of-control spray-tanning booth, dodging mind-inducing injections, and almost dying in a scorching sweat lodge were just a few of the awful things that we'd endured at Roland's. We'd had some pretty dangerous times at the so-called retreat and spa. But thankfully, all that was over.

"There's no cult in that mansion anymore, Bess," I said.

"And Roland is dead," George added.

As we neared Stacey's beach, we saw a group of people cleaning up. They introduced themselves as a team of environmentalists, some still in college.

"Can we help?" I asked.

"Thanks," a guy wearing a baseball cap said. He pointed to a box of disposable plastic gloves. "Just slip into those and get to work."

There was plenty to pick up and toss into garbage bags, including dead creatures of all types from clams to jellyfish, all injured by the spill. Bess was about to lift up an oil-slicked turtle when someone shouted, "We've got him, miss!"

A man and a woman, wearing identical white coveralls and gloves, walked over to us.

"We're from the local animal rescue organization," the woman explained in a friendly voice. "We'll take care of the turtle."

"We don't mind helping," I said.

"Everyone who works with our group has to be trained to handle injured animals," the man said. "Training can take weeks."

"We don't have that long," George said. "We're visiting from River Heights. That's in the—"

"Midwest," the man finished, nodding. He pointed to the blackened sand and said, "I'll bet you don't see stuff like this over there."

"Thankfully, no," I answered.

While the couple tended to the turtle, Bess asked, "Just curious, but did you ever work with the Blue Greenies?"

"Work with them?" the woman said with a snort. "The Blue Greenies have their *own* way of working on disasters."

"Yeah, like causing their own," the guy said.

After about two hours of picking up debris, we said good-bye to the environmentalists and the animal rescuers. We dumped our gloves in a trash can on the beach, then climbed the deck to Stacey's house.

"Stacey?" I called as we filed inside.

No answer.

"Where do you think she went?" Bess asked.

"She said she was giving a press conference for the party," I said, just remembering. "That Luellen must work pretty fast."

"I'll bet the press conference is next door at the mansion," George said. "Why don't we go over there and watch?"

Bess didn't look too thrilled to be going next door.

"Bess, are you okay?" I asked.

"Sure," she said with a nod. "If I'm going to be working on this party, I'd better deal with that mansion."

We decided to take the road to the mansion instead of walking along the beach, but as I opened the front door of Stacey's house and stepped out—

"Nancy, watch it!" George warned.

"What?" I asked, stopping in my tracks.

Bess and George stared down at the doorstep. I looked down too and froze. Splayed on the cement was an oil-covered seabird. A stiff and obviously dead seabird.

"The poor thing probably tried to fly and couldn't make it," Bess said in almost a whisper.

"Yeah, but how did he make it all the way from the ocean to the front of the house?" George wondered. "Especially in that condition."

I was wondering the same thing when a strong gust of wind ruffled the bird's sticky feathers. It uncovered something white underneath. I knelt down for a closer look.

"You guys, there's something tied around the dead bird's neck," I said slowly. "It looks like some kind of . . . note."

# CLUES AND DÉJÀ VUS

"**W**ho would put a note around a bird's neck?" Bess asked. "A *dead* bird's neck? Come on, we have to read it."

"I'm not touching a dead animal without gloves on," I said.

Bess grabbed a twig and gave it to George. "Here," she said. "Use this to flip the note open."

"Why do I always have to do the dirty work?" George said, but she took the stick and opened the paper.

I read out loud:

*Roses are red.*
*Violets are blue.*
*Watch your step—*
*Our eyes are on you.*

"No signature," I said.

"That's because whoever wrote it is a lousy poet," George said with a frown. "Roses are red, violets are blue—how original."

"Who cares about the poem?" Bess said nervously. "The note's some kind of warning—for Stacey or for us."

But who would want to warn *us*?

"It says *our* eyes are watching," I said, further studying the message. "So maybe there's more than one person behind this."

Our detective instincts kicked in as we started looking for clues. Around the side of the house George found a trail of wet footprints—but not like any feet we had seen before. They looked like huge duck feet. Or the kind of flippers divers and swimmers wore.

"Hey, weren't Cassie and Nathan wearing flippers when we met them on the beach?" George asked.

"Yes, but why would the Blue Greenies leave Stacey or us a warning?" Bess asked.

"For the same reason they launched that coffin,"

George said. "Creeping people out and making trouble in the name of their cause is what they do."

"They also saw how freaked out we were by that coffin," I said. "They probably wanted to have some more fun at our expense."

"Let's be glad they didn't set fire to the house," George said, shaking her head. "That's another of their warped methods."

We tracked down the animal rescuers we'd met earlier on the beach, and while it was too late to save the bird, they promised to dispose of it carefully and respectfully.

After scrubbing down the doorstep and sweeping the path, we were ready to go next door.

"To be honest," I said as we walked through the open gate of Roland's defunct retreat, "I never thought we'd be back here either."

Once inside, Bess, George, and I expected to find a press conference going on. Instead we saw a flurry of people hauling ladders, cans of paint, and brushes. One guy was holding papers that looked like construction plans.

"What's going on?" I wondered.

Stacey walked into view, staring down at her phone. "Hello, girls," she said as her thumbs busily texted. "I was just adding a few things to my schedule."

When *wasn't* Stacey glued to her phone and her schedule?

"Hi, Stacey," I said. "Who are all these—"

"Malachite Morning Show, six o'clock a.m.," Stacey said to herself. She finally looked up and smiled. "Guess what? Thanks to my press conference, the buzz on the party has begun. You wouldn't believe the interviews I've set up—morning shows, newscasts, social media—"

"Coming through!" a young guy shouted, barely missing Stacey with the ladder he was carrying.

"What's all this?" George asked.

But before Stacey could answer George, her phone blared and she shouted, "What do you mean you can't get me flowers from Bora-Bora?" Her voice trailed off as she walked away. "Do you know how many A-listers are coming to this event? Of course they can tell the difference!"

"And speaking of B-list celebs," George said, "here come Mandy and Mallory."

"George!" I hissed, jabbing her with my elbow.

Mandy and Mallory zigzagged around the workers toward us.

"Surprise!" Mallory exclaimed. "Mandy and I asked the show *House Busters* to get the mansion in shape for the party, and they came in a flash!"

"They're famous for that," Mandy said.

"*House Busters?*" Bess said. "You mean the reality show where they fix up houses at record-breaking speed?"

"Correct!" Mallory said, her eyes flashing. "The producer promised us they would fix up the mansion in just a few days—even redo the pool, too. Can you believe it?"

"I should have known it was another reality show," George said. She nodded at two buff guys carrying tool kits. "Those guys look like Abercrombie models with hammers."

"Don't worry, they're not bringing their cameras," Mandy said. "The cast and crew just want to help the beach out like everyone else."

"When they're finished, they'll film the reveal," Mallory added. "It's in their contract."

As Mallory spoke I noticed something weird. She was wearing shorts and a bikini top, but her stomach was covered with markings—as if someone had drawn on her skin with a pen.

"What's with the treasure map?" George asked.

Mallory looked down and giggled. "Oops, I meant to wash it off," she explained. "Right after the meeting I drove straight to Dr. Raymond's office. He was just showing me where I could use a little lipo."

"You mean liposuction?" I asked. "You don't need that, Mallory. You look great, really healthy."

"Healthy?" Mallory gasped. "That means fat, doesn't it?"

"Calm down," Mandy told her sister. She turned to us and smiled. "Mallory's not having liposuction. She talked to Dr. Raymond about a contest we thought of after the meeting."

"Yes!" Mallory said excitedly. "Whoever donates the most money to save the beach wins the plastic surgery procedure of their choice, performed by Dr. Raymond!"

"Genius!" Mandy said.

Mallory smiled. "We've got to go now," she said. "The landscapers are here, and we want to make sure they don't plant anything fake."

I started laughing as the sisters hurried off.

"Go figure," George said, shaking her head. "They don't want any fake plants, but they have no problem with fake chins—"

"George, give the sisters a break," Bess cut in. "They're doing the best they can to save the beach."

We walked through the house, dodging painters, carpenters, and designers. Work was going on all through the mansion—even in parts of the west wing where Roland's notorious cult had been housed.

"Talk about déjà vu," I said as we entered the all-too-familiar west wing. We approached the door to Inge's old office, and I grabbed the doorknob.

"Nancy, *what* are you doing?" Bess asked.

"I want to see if the *House Busters* crew got to this room yet," I said, opening the door.

With Bess and George behind me, I stepped inside. The room looked exactly the same as the day Inge signed Bess and me up for the cult. She'd had no clue we were there to investigate the retreat. But later she became suspicious, and that's when things started getting hairy.

"How's that for déjà vu?" George said, pointing to Roland's portrait hanging behind the desk.

I shivered as I gazed at the portrait. The cult leader's image was so lifelike with its cold blue eyes and grim smile.

"Okay, I know this might sound a little crazy," Bess said. "But I feel like the eyes in the portrait are watching us."

"Yup, it's crazy," George said with a nod.

The door to Roland's office was right off Inge's. It was shut too, but as I tried to open it—

"It's locked," I said. "Why would Inge's office be open and not Roland's?"

"Maybe the police locked it," Bess said with a shrug.

"I think we've spent enough time in here," George said, pulling me away from the door. "Let's leave this skeevy office already."

"I second the motion," Bess said. "Maybe we can help some of those guys fix up the mansion. I am good at fixing and building things, you know."

"*And* flirting," I teased. "Some of those guys *were* pretty hot."

We turned to leave Inge's office when—

*THUMP!!*

"What was that?" Bess asked softly.

"I don't know," I whispered back.

What I *did* know was where the noise had come from: Roland's office. His *locked* office.

# BEHIND CLOSED DOORS

I called through the door, "Anybody in there?"

We waited a good fifteen seconds for a response.

"Roland's body was never found," Bess said. "You do know that, don't you?"

"How can we forget, Bess?" George asked. "You keep reminding us every ten minutes."

The thought of Roland still alive and holed inside his office gave me a chill, but before I could try the doorknob again, George grabbed my hand.

"Forget the noise and forget Roland," George said. "Something heavy probably fell off a shelf or some furniture. Remember, there's a ton of construction going on in this place."

That did make sense to me. All that drilling and hammering would make even the strongest house shake and rattle.

"Let's go," I said, turning away from the door.

"Wait," George said. She walked over to Roland's portrait and took it off the wall. "Why should we have to look at his sorry face anymore?"

George placed the portrait on the floor, Roland's sinister face toward the wall. She dusted off her hands and said, "*Now* we can go!"

"We have a busy day ahead, girls," Stacey said after a sip of her mocha java. "Sending out the invites, ordering flowers, getting estimates from the limo companies . . ."

Half listening to her, I looked out on the beach. It had been two days since the Malachite meeting. We had never told Stacey about the strange note or the noise coming from Roland's office. Not that Stacey would have even heard us, the way she was focused on the party and her phone.

Cleanup crews were still working the beach, and I wished we were down there helping out instead of eating a leisurely breakfast, but Stacey insisted she needed our help today, especially today.

"Guess what?" Stacey's voice interrupted my

thoughts. "Thanks to those amazing House Busters, the renovations on the mansion should be ready by tomorrow."

"Have you come up with a date for the party?" Bess asked.

"I'm shooting for next Saturday night," Stacey said. "I know it's just a little over a week, but we can pull it off."

"What about the entertainment?" I asked. "And the food—"

"Done!" Stacey declared. "I just received two confirmations this morning. The first was Miss Zaza's manager to tell me that Zaza will perform at the event with two of her backup singers."

Even George looked excited at the news. Getting Miss Zaza for any party was huge!

"I can't believe we're going to meet the incredible Miss Z," Bess said.

"I can't believe she once wore a dress made of cooked lobsters," George said.

"Zaza assured me she will *not* be wearing her famous lobster number to the party," Stacey said. "Instead she'll be wearing an illuminated mermaid costume with a giant half shell. Which reminds me—"

She picked up her smartphone. "Ten a.m., schedule rehearsal time for Zaza," she said aloud as she entered the latest addition to her schedule. "Ten thirty a.m., order stretch limo . . . Now, doesn't this beat picking up stinky oil clumps and dead crabs?"

I blinked at Stacey's question. There was no comparison between a party and a disastrous oil spill.

"This might be more fun," I admitted. "But not necessarily more important—"

"Waiters!" Stacey interrupted.

"Huh?" I asked.

"I can't believe I forgot to hire waiters for the party," Stacey said, grabbing her phone again.

"My mom usually lines up a catering service for her parties," George said. "They handle the food and the waitstaff."

"Catering service—how River Heights!" Stacey said with a snort. "For this party I got Chef André Walters to create some of his famous recipes. That was my second confirmation."

"André Walters?" Bess asked. "He's the hottest celebrity chef these days. How did you get him?"

Stacey grinned and said, "I just happen to roll with a fabulous crowd."

I heard George sigh. What Stacey had said about her mom *was* kind of tacky.

"Oh, and I'll need you to do something else for me, if you don't mind," Stacey went on as she added another item to her schedule.

"Sure, what is it?" I asked.

"Can you move into the mansion next door until the party's over?" Stacey asked with a smile. "The bedrooms have just been finished, and I hear they're fabulous."

Had she just asked us to move out of her house into Roland's old mansion?

She continued, "You would have the whole mansion to yourselves. I'll even make sure the fridge is stocked."

"Um," I said. "That sounds nice, Stacey, but—"

"But why do you want us to move out of your house?" George finished for me.

"Nothing personal," Stacey blurted. "It's just that the closer I get to an event, the more peace and quiet I need at home. You know, my office is here in the house."

I couldn't imagine frenetic Stacey needing any peace and quiet. I was about to promise to be quiet when George piped up.

"Sure, Stacey," she said. "If that's what you want, we'll move next door."

Bess stared at George, horrified. "After what happened to Nancy and me over there?" she said. "I wouldn't stay at that mansion for all the money in the world."

"Does that mean no?" Stacey asked.

Her eyes were still on Bess as she answered an

incoming call. I wasn't crazy about moving next door either, but it seemed important to George.

"Meeting," George whispered to us.

As we walked to the steps of the deck, Bess said, "Don't bother talking me into it, George. I am not moving into that mansion. Period."

"I don't really want to move there either," I admitted. "I mean, why can't we just stay here? We're already unpacked."

"Because Stacey was nice enough to invite us to Malachite Beach," George said. "Now that she needs her privacy, I think we should let her have it."

"What about our awful experience?" Bess said.

"After the House Busters get through with that mansion, it'll look like a totally different place," George said.

"On the outside," Bess groaned under her breath.

What had happened at Roland's was still pretty fresh in my mind—but the thought of having a whole Malachite mansion to ourselves, I had to admit, was pretty sweet.

"It could be fun," I said with a shrug. "Think of all that awesome food Stacey is promising us."

"Okay, but what about that strange thumping noise we heard the other day?" Bess said. "How would you like to hear *that* in the middle of the night?"

"The construction work caused that noise," I

said, still hoping it was true. "We figured that out, remember?"

"Getting out of Stacey's hair is a good idea," George said. "My mom is a raging lunatic right before one of her events. Can you imagine how nuts Stacey gets right before a party?"

The three of us glanced at Stacey pacing back and forth while shouting on her phone.

"Come to think of it," Bess said with a smile, "maybe we'd *better* move into that mansion."

"Yes!" said George. She slapped Bess playfully on the back, almost knocking her off the deck.

Stacey had just finished her call as we walked back to the breakfast table.

"We'll be happy to move next door, Stacey," I said. "Just tell us when you'd like us to do it."

"How about right now?" she said.

"Now?" I repeated, not expecting the urgency.

"Yes. And so you can continue to help me and focus on the party, I hired a housekeeper named Olga to clean up the mansion while you're there," Stacey added.

She glanced down at her phone. "Olga arrives at three p.m.," she said aloud, adding it to her schedule.

"Stacey, you don't have to spend money on a housekeeper for us," George said. "We clean up after ourselves."

"Olga said she'll work the event for free," Stacey said. "She told me over the phone that she's really into saving the beach and wants to do whatever she can to help."

"Nice," I said.

We sat and chatted awhile longer, finishing our coffee, croissants, fruit, and yogurt.

"I had no idea you were so traumatized by Roland's cult," Stacey said, taking another sip of coffee. "How are you girls holding up?"

*Other than the dead bird on our doorstep, the creepy note around its neck, and the weird bump we heard yesterday?* I thought.

"We're fine," I said aloud. "Now that we're going to be involved with this amazing party, even better."

Stacey took a final sip of coffee and stood up. "I'm going next door to meet with the *House Busters* crew. You girls can start packing, if you don't mind doing the dishes first."

"Where is this Olga when we need her?" George joked. But in record time, we cleared the table, loaded the dishwasher, swept the deck, and sponged down the table. Then we went to our rooms to pack.

I opened my suitcase on the bed, then grabbed my clothes from the closet and dresser and jammed everything in. I was about to toss in the T-shirt I'd bought in Santa Monica when I noticed the price tag still dangling from it.

I rummaged through my makeup bag for a pair of scissors to snip off the tag, but couldn't find them.

So I went to Stacey's home office, opened the top drawer of her desk, and found rubber bands, paper clips, pens, and a tube of berry lip balm, but no scissors.

*Come on, Stacey. You're all about the details. How can you not have scissors?* I thought, and pulled the drawer open some more. Success—a pair was in the back, on top of a hardcover book.

I picked the scissors up and gasped. Staring up at me was *Roland*!

Omigod! It was Roland's book, *You Are That!*

I opened it, and the first thing I saw on the title page was a handwritten note: *To Stacey. Thank you for being such a dear, dear friend. Yours always, Roland.*

My eyes stayed glued to the page. I read the note twice more. What was Roland's book doing inside Stacey's desk—and why did he call her his *friend*?

"Bess, George!" I shouted. "Get in here—NOW!"

# MYSTERIOUS MANSION

In a flash Bess and George were with me in Stacey's office. When I showed them Roland's personal note to Stacey, they couldn't believe it either.

"Stacey told us she barely knew Roland," Bess said. "So what's up with this?"

"Kind of weird, huh?" I said.

"Maybe," George said. "Or maybe not."

"What do you mean?" I asked.

"Maybe Stacey was being a good neighbor," George said. "She could have helped Roland when he first moved in. Maybe she planned an event or party for him and the book was his way of saying thanks."

"With a little self-promotion, perhaps?" I asked.

"Exactly," George said. "I'll bet Stacey never even read his dumb book."

She then stuck the book back into the drawer and slammed it shut. "Come on. Let's finish packing."

Bess and George left Stacey's office. It was hard for me not to look at Roland's book as I opened the drawer again for the scissors. This time I noticed something else—the top edge of a red bookmark peeking out from the pages.

Once again I pulled the book out and opened it to where it was marked, right before the fifth chapter, "Success at Any Cost." If Stacey was reading Roland's book, had she gotten that far? I knew Roland believed in success at any cost, but did Stacey?

"Nancy?" Bess shouted to me from her room. "Have you seen my purple flip-flops?"

I slammed the book shut and slipped it inside the drawer again. "I think they're on the deck, Bess," I called as I finally snipped off the T-shirt's price tag.

Leaving Stacey's office, I decided not to tell Bess and George about the bookmark.

*Roland could have put it there himself,* I told myself. *To point out his favorite chapter.*

George and I finished packing in less than half an hour. Bess needed more time to fill up two suitcases and a duffel bag.

We finally left Stacey's house, pleased to see no more dead birds or menacing notes on the doorstep. Bess lagged behind, grunting from the weight of her bags, as we rolled our luggage down the road to the mansion.

"What'd you do, Bess?" George called back to her. "Bring your whole closet from River Heights?"

"We're in L.A. for three weeks," Bess grunted. "Three times seven equals twenty-one different outfits, plus extras for evening. Do the math."

When we reached the mansion, the front door was wide open. We left our luggage in the entrance hall and stepped farther inside.

I could see Stacey flitting around and shouting last-minute suggestions to the House Busters. She didn't seem like the type who would fall under the spell of a crazy cult leader like Roland. There *had* to be an explanation for Roland's book.

"Hi, guys!" a voice said.

I turned around to see Alice hurrying by, holding a can of paint in one hand.

"Helping out here today, Alice?" I asked.

"Just for the morning, before I help clean the beach," Alice said. She lowered her voice to a whisper. "You are not going to believe who else showed up to help."

I looked to see where Alice was nodding. There, standing next to a ladder and handing a hammer up to a carpenter, was Austin Gruber.

"After the way Stacey spoke to him at that meeting, you'd think he'd never show his face," George said.

Alice had already left to deliver the can to the painter. When Austin looked our way, he smiled and walked over.

"Hey," he said, his cheeks turning pink. Although the greeting was meant for all of us, his eyes were on Bess.

"Hi, Austin," Bess said, and smiled back.

"We didn't think we'd see you here," I said.

"How come?" Austin asked.

This time I blushed. "Um . . . well, after the way Stacey . . . you know—"

"Spoke to you like you were some five-year-old kid," George finished for me.

"I know, but it's still my beach," Austin said, flashing Bess a tiny smile. "I want to do whatever I can to pitch in."

I smiled too. Maybe Austin was as nice as he was cute. And I had to admit he was cute!

"That's really awesome of you, Austin," Bess said.

"You think?" Austin asked softly. He seemed so shy that I couldn't believe he sang in front of thousands of teenage girls on a regular basis.

"Um." Austin nodded to the luggage we'd dropped in the entrance hall. "Can I help you carry those bags somewhere?"

I was about to thank Austin when Stacey raced over.

"Drop whatever you're doing, girls," Stacey said. "Miss Zaza is coming here to the mansion tonight to rehearse her big number."

"Seriously?" Bess gasped. "We're going to get to meet Miss Z *tonight*?"

"Miss Z . . . six p.m. . . . ," Stacey said, entering the rehearsal time in her phone. "Miss Zaza is also bringing the mermaid costume she's planning on performing in. The one with a giant shell that lights up."

Austin muttered something under his breath, but I couldn't quite hear it.

"I want to hold the dress rehearsal upstairs," Stacey said. "There's plenty of room up in Roland's old sanctuary."

Had she said "sanctuary"? I knew the huge room upstairs had been called Roland's sanctuary—but how did she know?

"Maybe Austin here can help Miss Zaza during the rehearsal," Stacey went on, pointing a finger at him. "You know, like bring her water or coffee, that kind of stuff."

"Uh-oh," George murmured.

"I figured Miss Zaza would feel comfortable around you," Stacey told him. "Since you're a performer too."

Austin pretended to be surprised. "I am?" he asked. "Thanks for reminding me—I almost forgot."

"Super," said Stacey. "I'll add you to the schedule: Five thirty, Austin to set out sandwich and fruit platter . . . five forty-five, Austin make coffee . . . one urn decaf."

Stacey looked up at Bess, George, and me. "The bedrooms upstairs in the west wing have been totally refurbished," she said. "Choose any you want and make yourselves at home."

"Thanks," I said.

Austin was almost seething as Stacey walked away, her phone pressed to her ear.

"Oh, well," he said. "If Her Majesty is arriving soon, I'd better start rolling out the red carpet." And he walked away.

"Too awkward," George said.

"I can't believe Stacey had the audacity to treat Austin Gruber that way," Bess said. "Doesn't she know who he is?"

That wasn't the only thing that bothered me.

"Did you hear how Stacey called the upstairs room Roland's 'sanctuary'?" I asked.

Bess's eyes widened. "That's what Roland and Inge

called it," she said. "How would Stacey know that if she hardly knew her neighbors?"

"Exactly," I said.

I was about to tell them about the bookmark in Stacey's copy of *You Are That* when George said, "Not for nothing, Nancy, but I really think you're thinking too much."

"And you aren't?" I asked.

"Not as much as you," George said. "I even forgot about the dead bird and the creepy note on our doorstep."

"Me too . . . until you just reminded me," Bess said.

So I decided not to bring up the bookmark, at least for now. George seemed to be protective of Stacey, probably because the event planner knew her mom.

We took our bags and hurried past the *House Busters* crew, who were putting the finishing touches on the mansion. Gone were the heavy furniture, darkly painted walls, and iron candle sconces. Now the same walls were a cool aqua with white trim. But the real surprise came when we opened the doors to our bedrooms. . . .

"Epic!" Bess exclaimed.

Bess and I walked into the exact same room we'd used during our cult investigation—and I hardly recognized it.

"Look," Bess said, pointing to the beds. "This time there's bedding."

I smiled at the elegantly made beds, strewn with satiny pillows. Roland's cult had not allowed any bedding—not even pillows—in order to discourage sleep.

"We've got a TV, too," I said, pointing to a sleek flat-screen on the wall.

George was fine with having her own room next door. She was already in there unpacking.

"Let's check out George's room," Bess said. "While it's still clean."

Before Bess and I could head for the door, we heard a knock. We jumped, but then we giggled.

"I bet it's George," I said. "She probably wants to see our room."

I opened the door and my mouth dropped open. A tall, unfamiliar woman was standing there.

Her hair was long—long and *bright* orange. One side hung over her face like a curtain, brushing against a bulbous nose. I couldn't see her eyes because they were hidden by thick black sunglasses, but I could feel them piercing through me.

"Um," I said, my mouth dry. "May I help you?"

# DOOM SERVICE

**B**y now Bess was peering over my shoulder at the strange woman.

"Towels," the woman mumbled. She lifted a basket filled with folded towels and bars of soap. "For your room and your friend's."

I took the towels from the woman, and then it finally clicked. . . .

"Oh!" I said with a smile. "You must be—"

"Olga," the woman mumbled. Without another word, she turned and shuffled down the hall.

Bess and I leaned out the door, watching Olga until she disappeared down the staircase.

"That's the housekeeper Stacey hired?" I asked. "The one who was so passionate about saving the beach that she'd work for free?"

"She doesn't seem like the passionate type to me. Maybe she's just eccentric," Bess said.

"Or weird," I said.

We checked out George's room, which was as nice as ours, then went downstairs to help Stacey with the party planning.

The first thing she had us do was send out the invites, which had arrived from the printer. We sat in the newly renovated dining room, stuffing envelopes, then sticking preprinted labels on them.

"How amazing is this?" Bess said, waving a sheet of labels in the air. "These are the addresses of just about every A-list celebrity in Hollywood."

I looked up in time to see Austin walking past the door. He slowed when he saw Bess, but when he caught my eye, he blushed and hurried on.

After finishing the invites, we ordered the flowers Stacey wanted for the party. I couldn't believe I was calling the island of Bora-Bora in the South Pacific.

"So this is the glam life of an event planner," I said after making the call.

"Glamorous?" George said. "Tell that to my mom when she's rushing a melting ice cream cake to a party of screaming three-year-olds."

It was close to dinnertime when our stomachs started to growl. We were eating cold leftover pizza from the House Busters' lunch when Stacey appeared in the doorway.

"She's here, she's here!" Stacey cried. "Miss Zaza's limo has arrived."

We jumped up from our chairs and raced out of the kitchen to the front door. Stacey was standing at the end of the driveway, waving to a parked stretch limo. As a chauffeur opened the back door, Bess named each passenger as they stepped out of the car.

"The man in the black suit is Kurt Lambert, Miss Zaza's manager," Bess said in a low voice. "The woman in the long gypsy skirt and tank top is her choreographer. I think her name is Suki."

"Who are those two guys?" I asked of the tall, slim pair who filed out of the car.

Bess didn't miss a beat. "Brad and Russell—Miss Zaza's backup singers."

"There's Mandy!" I cut in as Mandy Casabian stepped out of the limo next. She was dressed in a white pantsuit with Western fringes and silver studs.

Miss Zaza's entourage waited silently. And then, one leg wearing green fishnet tights and a tasseled mini-boot slowly emerged from the car door.

"It's her!" Bess squealed.

The leg was soon followed by the entire body of Miss Zaza.

"How cool is that?" I whispered.

Stacey's arms waved excitedly as she spoke to Miss Zaza. I couldn't hear what Stacey was saying, but I could see what Miss Zaza was wearing—a forest-green cape and feathered cap that reminded me of Robin Hood.

"If I knew it was Halloween, I would have brought candy," a voice muttered.

We turned. Austin was standing behind us. He was about to take a sip from a plastic water bottle when Stacey called, "Austin, come give us a hand."

Austin sighed. He stuck the bottle inside his jacket pocket, then brushed past us to join the others. It wasn't long before he was unloading Miss Zaza's costume from the trunk.

"We'd better go help him," I said as Austin buckled under the giant half shell.

The moment Mandy saw us, she introduced us to Miss Zaza. The superstar smiled and said, "Nice to meet you."

Bess and I just grinned, too stunned to speak. George, on the other hand, had no trouble.

"Is Zaza your real name?" she asked.

Stacey seemed horrified by George's question, but Zaza didn't seem to mind.

"No, Zaza isn't my real name," she said. "I actually hate my real name. It's Zenobia, but don't tell anyone, especially the press."

"Hey, I hate my real name too," George said, surprised. "I guess we have more in common than I thought."

"Girls, girls," Stacey said, pushing us toward the limo. "Why don't you help Austin with Miss Zaza's costume?"

I could see Austin grinning at Bess as she happily lifted Miss Zaza's towering platform shoes from the trunk.

He carried Miss Zaza's giant half shell while I carefully cradled the mermaid costume, heavy with hundreds of tiny bulbs sewn to the fabric. George ran to help Austin shimmy the gigantic shell through the front door.

"It could have been worse," George grunted as they struggled with the shell. "She could have brought her stinky lobster dress."

Stacey whisked Miss Zaza and company into the living room and called to us, "Bring everything upstairs to the sanctuary, please!"

"I wish she'd stop calling it the sanctuary," Bess whispered to me.

"*We'll* call it the rehearsal hall," I said.

Lugging Miss Zaza's gear to the west wing and

up the spiral staircase wasn't easy, but the effort was worth it. We found state-of-the-art audio equipment set up for her rehearsal. Even a rolling garment rack for her costume stood before the small stage.

All traces of Roland's cult were gone—like the velvet "throne" he'd sat on as he stared down his followers.

George and Austin placed the giant shell on the stage. Bess carefully stood Miss Zaza's shoes on the floor beside the rack where I struggled to hang the heavy, elaborate mermaid costume.

"Look at all these tiny bulbs sewn onto the costume," I said once the costume was up.

"Allow me to demonstrate how it works," Austin said. Reaching around it, he flipped a tiny switch located near the zipper. Soon the bulbs began blinking and twinkling. "Ta-da! I could see the switch from where I was standing."

"How does it work?" I asked. "It's not like it has a cord to plug in."

"It was probably electrically charged before it was brought here," I heard Bess say. "If you think that's neat, check this out."

Bess towered over us—a whole foot taller than her usual height. I glanced down to see Miss Zaza's shoes on *Bess's* feet!

"Get out of those shoes before Miss Zaza or Stacey

see you," I warned Bess. "Then let's go downstairs. Maybe Stacey will let us sit in on the meeting."

Austin held Bess's hand as she carefully stepped out of the shoes. Then he said, "You guys go ahead downstairs. I want to hang out up here for a while and take some pictures of Zaza's costume." He pulled out his phone. "Some of my buds are Zaza fans."

I didn't like the idea of leaving Austin alone with Zaza's things. After all, he wasn't exactly a Zaza fan himself. Quite the opposite, it seemed.

"Stacey might want to keep the costume a secret," I told Austin.

"Nancy, relax," Bess said. "It's not like he's sending the pictures to AMZ."

I still felt uncomfortable about Austin being alone with Miss Zaza's costume. But maybe George was right. Maybe I was thinking too much.

"Okay," I told Austin. "Just be quick and don't let Stacey see you."

"Yes, ma'am!" Austin said, giving me a little salute. He gave Bess one last smile before we filed down the staircase.

When we reached the living room, the meeting was going strong. Miss Zaza was sitting on the sofa, daintily nibbling on a sandwich. Stacey was pacing back and forth in front of Zaza's manager, Kurt, a coffee cup in her hand.

"Let me get this straight," Kurt said. "Zaza is going to be singing on the beach?"

"The dirty beach?" Zaza asked, wrinkling her nose.

"Your feet will never touch the sand," Stacey promised. "Starting tomorrow, we'll be constructing a stage just for the event—with a full sound system and lights."

Bess, George, and I were about to sit on a brand-new divan when Stacey said, "Now, if we're all finished here, I'd like to show you our rehearsal space."

*Oh no,* I thought. What if Austin was still photographing Miss Zaza's dress?

"Um . . . we have a few questions about the party," I blurted.

"Can they wait?" Stacey asked as they exited the living room. "We really have to run through Zaza's number."

The three of us fell behind as Stacey led the others toward the staircase.

"At least Stacey didn't call it the sanctuary this time," Bess whispered.

"I just hope Austin is finished," I said. "I knew we shouldn't have left him upstairs alone."

But once we were upstairs, Austin Gruber was nowhere to be found.

"Where'd he go?" I whispered.

"Who knows? At least he wasn't caught taking

pictures," George said. "That's what you were worried about, remember?"

That—and leaving Austin alone with Miss Zaza's costume.

Mandy waved us over to the stage, where Suki was choreographing and explaining Miss Zaza's number. "The backup singers enter first in darkness, then the lights come up and Zaza will make her grand entrance."

"Let's do this!" Miss Zaza said, whipping off her green cape. Underneath she wore a one-piece leotard perfect for slinking into a tight costume.

"Nancy, Bess, George?" Stacey called. "Can you help Zaza into her costume, please?"

We carefully slipped the costume off the rack, then held it while Miss Zaza stepped into it. Next we lifted the heavy shell, holding it steady until Zaza slipped her arms through the attached straps. When Miss Z was fully costumed, Suki flicked the switch. Stacey gasped with delight as the tiny bulbs blinked, twinkled, and flashed.

"Wait," Bess called out excitedly. "Don't forget your shoes."

Bess hurried over to the shoes near the clothing rack, and as she carried them to Miss Zaza, I noticed two wet footprints on the floor—wet spots left by the shoes!

I started to panic as I did the math: Wet shoes . . . plus electric costume . . . equals disaster!

"Stop—Zaza, stop!" I shouted. "Don't dare step into those shoes!"

# ON THE HEELS OF DANGER

All eyes were on me as I raced over to Miss Zaza.

"Nancy, what are you doing?" Stacey said when I snatched the shoe out from under Miss Zaza's foot.

Without saying a word, I tipped the shoe upside down—and water poured out onto the floor.

Everyone stared while I grabbed Miss Zaza's other shoe from her. I didn't need to tip it over to see a small amount of water sloshing around inside.

"My shoes were filled with *water*?" Miss Zaza asked as I flicked off her flashing costume.

"Omigosh," Mandy said, flipping her hair over her shoulder. "I'm not a scientist, but I know not to blow-dry my hair near water. That's dangerous, right?"

"Try fatal," I said. "If Zaza had stepped into those shoes with wet feet, she could have been electrocuted."

Stunned whispers filled the room, but my thoughts turned to Austin. Had he really taken pictures? Or had he taken his bottle of water to Miss Zaza's shoes?

"How did water get inside her shoes, Stacey?" Kurt demanded. "They were bone-dry when I packed them."

"The shoes *were* dry," Bess said. "At least they were dry when I tried them on."

Silence.

"Uh-oh," George said under her breath.

"You tried on my shoes?" Miss Zaza asked, more surprised than angry.

Bess turned bright red when she realized her mistake. "Um . . . I . . . I—," she started to say, but didn't get very far.

"Hold on." Stacey looked from me to Bess to George. "Didn't I ask you girls to carry Miss Zaza's costume up here before?"

*Us . . . and Austin Gruber,* I thought, but kept my mouth shut.

"Wait a minute, Stacey," George said. "Are you accusing us of trying to harm Miss Zaza?"

"Well," Stacey said frostily. She nodded at the platforms. "If the shoe fits . . ."

"Stacey, that's crazy," I said. "If we wanted to hurt Zaza, why would I have stopped her from putting on her shoes?"

Stacey looked at me, unable to answer.

"Well, somebody tried to hurt Zaza," Brad, the backup singer, said. "I'm not sure I want to perform at this party."

"Me neither," Russell agreed.

Kurt turned to Stacey. "As Zaza's manager, I have to decide if we're participating in this fund-raiser," he said. "I'll call you tomorrow with my answer."

Stacey looked devastated. "Kurt, wait! I'm sure there's an explanation for this," she cried as she chased Zaza and her entourage down the staircase.

Mandy turned to us, her face dark with anger. "Good job, you guys," she said sarcastically.

"Don't tell me *you* think we poured water in Miss Zaza's shoes," George said angrily.

"I'm not saying you did it," Mandy explained. "You just should have been paying more attention to Miss Zaza's costume, that's all."

"Mandy, we were told to take the costume upstairs," Bess said. "Not to guard it."

"*Somebody* got to those shoes," Mandy said as she

headed to the staircase. "It's too bad my crew wasn't here to film all this. From now on I'm not going anywhere without them."

We watched as Mandy wound down the stairs. I was about to share my thoughts about Austin when Bess said, "Maybe Zaza uses insoles that are filled with liquid? They could have leaked, no?"

We examined the insides of Miss Zaza's shoes. No insoles—or clues anywhere.

"Okay, you guys," I said. "There's an eight-hundred-pound gorilla in the room."

"Is the gorilla's name Austin?" Bess asked. "I thought of him myself but didn't want to believe it."

"Austin *did* want to be alone with the costume," George added. "And he left before everyone got here." She walked over to the stage and leaned against it.

Just then I spotted a plastic water bottle with a Bubbling Brooks Water label, right near George.

"There's Austin's water bottle," I said. "He must have left it here."

Bess shook her head and said, "How could squeaky-clean Austin Gruber do anything so evil?"

I couldn't imagine the baby-faced singer doing anything evil either, but Austin did have a motive, and a pretty big one.

"Austin was dumped by Stacey for Miss Zaza," I

said. "Sabotaging her costume could have been his way of getting revenge. Or maybe he was hoping Miss Zaza would drop out so Stacey would replace her with him."

"Drop out or drop *dead*?" George said. "The artist formerly known as Zenobia could have been killed."

I wish I knew more about Austin and what made him tick. Then suddenly—a brainstorm!

"What are you doing, Nancy?" Bess asked as I pulled out my phone. "Calling the police?"

"I'm contacting Alice," I said. "She gave me her number back at the meeting."

"Why her?" George asked, surprised.

"Because Alice told us to ask her anything about Malachite or its residents," I said. "I think I'll ask her about Austin."

I texted Alice: WHAT DO U KNOW ABOUT AUSTIN GRUBER?

I pressed send and waited. Alice answered in record time. Bess and George looked over my shoulder as we read the reply together: R U KIDDING ME? AUSTIN IS THE NICEST BOY ON EARTH. ☺ HE'S KIND TO ANIMALS, VOLUNTEERS AT CHILDREN'S HOSPITALS. OK, HE'S SHY AROUND GIRLS SO HE HAS NO GIRLFRIEND. YET. I HOPE SOMEDAY IT'S ME!

I smiled at the text. Alice made Austin sound like he wouldn't even hurt a fly.

"Austin can't be the culprit, you guys," Bess said. "I mean, he volunteers at children's hospitals."

"Culprit, no," George agreed. "Suspect, yes."

I glanced at the doomed shoes, still damp with water.

"Here's a thought," I said. "What if the person who did this didn't want to kill Zaza? What if he or she wanted to kill the event?"

"Why would anyone want to kill an event to save the beach?" Bess asked.

"Yeah," George said. "It's all for the good."

"All I know is that somebody is out to sabotage this party," I said. "And we're going to find out who—before he or she strikes again."

"Good night, Olga," I called.

Bess and I stood in the doorway, watching the quirky housekeeper walk out of the gate. In the moonlight I could see Olga nod her head.

"Doesn't she have a car?" Bess asked. "I mean, doesn't everybody in California drive everywhere?"

"Olga isn't exactly everybody," I said. "Who knows? Maybe she lives within walking distance."

I closed the door, making sure to lock it. It was going to be our first night alone in the mansion.

"We'd better make sure *all* the doors are locked," I said.

"I already did," George said, joining us in the entrance hall. "I locked some windows, too—the ones with ledges wide enough to climb."

The thought of someone climbing through a window in the middle of the night made my skin crawl—but I refused to obsess.

"Do you think we should check the other rooms?" Bess asked.

"No," George said. "Stacey left, Olga left. No one is in the mansion except us."

We had planned to look for more clues about Zaza's shoes, but our cushy new beds were calling to us.

"Remember, George," Bess said when we reached our rooms. "If you get scared alone in your room tonight, just come in."

"Oh, puh-leeze," George groaned as she shut her door.

Once I was in bed, my head sank into the marshmallow-soft pillow, but my thoughts turned to Stacey.

After watching her today, I couldn't imagine her joining any kind of cult. She had an incredible event-planning career, a beach house on Malachite—why would she need a crazy associate like Roland to prop her up?

With that thought, I fell into a deep sleep. . . .

"Nancy, wake up!"

"Huh?" Bess was shaking my shoulder. As I peered through the darkness, I saw her face staring down at me.

"Did you hear that?" Bess hissed.

"Hear what?" I groaned.

"Listen," she whispered. "It sounds like someone's downstairs."

I groggily sat up in bed but heard nothing. I was about to tell Bess to go back to sleep when I heard a noise.

"What was that?" I said.

"It sounds like somebody is creeping around the house," Bess whispered. "I told you we shouldn't have stayed here overnight."

"Calm down," I said. "It's probably George sneaking leftover sandwiches from the kitchen. She always gets hungry in the middle of the night."

I turned on the bedside lamp and climbed out of bed.

"Where are you going?" Bess asked.

"Downstairs," I said, heading toward the door. "I'm kind of hungry myself. I'll keep her company."

But when I opened our bedroom door, I ran into George coming out of *her* room.

"Uh-oh," Bess said.

"You heard it too?" George asked.

"We were hoping it was you," I said, but then had

a thought. "It could be Stacey. Maybe she couldn't sleep, so she came back here to take care of stuff."

"That sounds like Stacey," George said as we made our way down the stairs.

The clattering stopped when we approached the staircase, but as we headed downstairs, the air suddenly became thick.

Omigod—smoke!

"You guys," I said, my heart beginning to pound, "the mansion's on fire!"

# PLAYING WITH FIRE

**W**e thundered down the stairs to see the front door wide open. Through the smoke-filled entrance hall I saw a fire burning on the hardwood floor near the door. It looked small, but the winds coming from outside were causing it to grow by the second.

I felt the blood drain from my face as I frantically weighed our options: run out and call the fire department or try putting the fire out ourselves. Since we didn't have our phones, I went for plan number two.

"Shut the door!" I shouted.

I darted past the flames to a window in the entrance

hall. "Help me with this!" I yelled, trying to pull the heavy curtain down.

George yanked the curtain, sending it—and the rod—crashing to the floor. Gathering the material in my arms, I ran toward the fire and threw the thick curtain over it, covering it completely. Bess and George followed my lead, patting at the material to smother the flames.

The smoke began to die down, and carefully I lifted the curtain to make sure the fire was out. All that was left were the remains of a charred rag—a rag I was sure had been first soaked with some kind of flammable liquid.

"Somebody set this fire," George said. "If we hadn't come down in time, we would have been killed."

"The most important thing is that we did," I said. "The second most important—who threw the flaming rag into the house?"

"The Blue Greenies are into burning mansions," George said angrily. "That rag could have been their calling card."

I opened the door and checked the lock.

"There's no sign of breaking in," I said. "Whoever opened the door must have used a key—and the Blue Greenies definitely have no key."

"We're the only ones with keys to the mansion," George said. "Us and Stacey."

"And Roland . . . and Inge," Bess murmured.

George snapped, "Bess, what part of 'Roland is dead and Inge is in jail' don't you get?"

"If you say so," Bess said. "Shouldn't we let the police know what happened?"

I gave it serious thought. The citizen in me said to call the police. The detective in me said to hold off.

"I'm not ready to call the police," I said. "If someone is determined to keep this event from happening, I'm just as determined to find out who it is."

We checked the room for burning embers, put the ruined curtain outside near the trash, and headed back upstairs.

"We'll tell Stacey about the fire in the morning," I said. "In the meantime, let's try to get some sleep."

"In this crazy place?" Bess said with a shudder. "Good luck!"

As I slipped back into bed, I wondered about the noises we'd heard earlier. They sounded like more than just a front door being opened—they sounded as if someone was inside and rummaging around the house.

The thought was troubling but not troubling enough to keep me awake.

The next morning I woke up, not to Bess's panicky voice, but to the awesome aroma of breakfast wafting up from downstairs, along with lively conversation and laughter.

*Wow,* I thought, remembering the crazy night before. *What a difference a day makes.*

I shook Bess awake and called George's cell to wake her up too. Ten minutes later we headed downstairs to the dining room.

"And I thought I liked to sleep in," Mandy's voice said.

I turned to see all three Casabian sisters sitting at the dining room table eating breakfast—but nothing like scrambled eggs or toast. The sisters were feasting on what looked like fried shrimp, tilapia fillets, and fresh grilled tuna steaks.

Circling them like buzzards was the crew of the sisters' reality show, *Chillin' with the Casabians.*

"Mia," the producer Bev barked, "make some kind of comment about how you thought tuna only came in cans."

"I will not pretend to be dumb, Bev," Mia said, rolling her eyes. "Now can you please leave us alone and let us eat our breakfast?"

"You call that breakfast?" George asked.

Stacey flitted into the room, staring at her phone. "There you are," she said. "You know, I didn't think you girls were smokers."

"Smokers?" I said.

"We don't smoke!" Bess insisted.

"Then what was that smell when I came into the house this morning?" Stacey asked.

"Last night, somebody broke into the house," I said. "They—"

But Stacey cut me off. "We're trying out Chef André Walters's dishes for the party." She smiled past my shoulder. "In fact, here he is now."

Chef Walters swept into the dining room, wearing a white jacket and a traditional chef toque. I recognized him from the pictures on his special seafood sauce labels.

"André asked Mandy, Mallory, and Mia to taste the food he's planning to prepare," Stacey said.

The jovial chef turned to us and smiled. "Ah!" he said, rubbing his hands together. "More guinea pigs to experiment on."

"He means grab a seat and eat!" Stacey said. She gestured to the table with her phone. "I hope you girls like seafood, because that's what's on the menu."

I did like seafood, but the thought of such heavy dishes first thing in the morning made my stomach churn. So did the camera that pointed directly at Bess, George, and me.

"Thanks," I said. "Maybe we'll have some leftovers later."

"That is," Chef Walters said with a wink at the camera, "if there are any leftovers!"

Bess took me aside and whispered, "Aren't we going to tell Stacey about the fire last night?"

"You saw," I whispered back. "I tried to tell her, but she cut me off. I'll try again later when there aren't so many people around."

"'Scuse me," a gruff voice said.

We turned to see Olga behind us, a platter of boiled lobster in her hands. As I watched her place the platter on the table, I noticed something odd: Her nose looked *crooked*.

My thoughts were interrupted, as usual, by Stacey. She came over and said, "No word yet from Miss Zaza or her manager, girls. Looks like we might have to settle for that young kid after all."

"You mean me?" Austin asked as he entered the room.

"Austin, there you are," Stacey said. "Try some of Chef Walters's dishes and tell me what you think. I'd like a boy's opinion."

"No problem," Austin said with a shrug.

Before he could head toward the table, George whispered, "Nancy, Bess, we have got to ask Austin about Miss Zaza."

"George!" Bess objected.

"She's right, Bess," I said. "Austin may be kind to animals and sick kids, but he's still a suspect."

Austin looked surprised as we stepped in front of him. "Hey. What's up?" he asked.

"We didn't see you at Miss Zaza's rehearsal last night," I said in a low voice.

"I know," Austin said coolly. "How did it go?"

"Other than Miss Zaza almost getting electrocuted?" George said, glaring at him.

*"Electrocuted?"* Austin said. "What happened?"

"Someone poured water into Miss Zaza's shoes," I said. "Zaza was wearing her electric costume when she almost stepped into them."

"Who do you think did it?" Austin asked. When we didn't answer, he looked straight at me and said, "Oh, come on. You don't think I did it—do you?"

"We found a half-empty water bottle near the shoes," George said. "You were carrying a bottle of water in your pocket."

"You mean this?" Austin said, pulling a bottle out of his jacket pocket. "It's the same one I had yesterday."

I noticed something about the bottle Austin was holding. The brand was Crystal Springs. The bottle we'd found last night had a Bubbling Brooks label.

"Why didn't we see you at Miss Zaza's rehearsal?" George asked.

"Because I took some pictures, then split," Austin replied. He glanced past us at Stacey. "I didn't want to hang around and be Zaza's gofer."

The pictures! Maybe they'd give us another clue.

"Can I see those pictures you took yesterday?" I asked.

"Sure," Austin said. He pulled out his phone and showed us six different pictures he'd taken of the costume next to a man in a navy-blue suit and hat.

"Austin, who is that?" I asked.

"Oh, that's Zaza's limo driver. He brought one last suitcase of hers upstairs, and we decided it would be fun to take a few photos with the outrageous costume—some with me and some with him. We left together right after that."

I smiled as I shook my head. I had seen enough. Enough for me to rule out Austin.

It seemed as though Bess was happiest of all. "Why didn't you say so, Austin? That limo driver is your alibi!"

"You know, I would never hurt anybody or anything," Austin said as he pocketed his phone. "I don't even like to swat mosquitoes or step on ants."

"My little sister Maggie says you're a real cool guy," Bess told Austin. "She's your biggest fan."

"Seriously?" Austin asked, smiling. "Um . . . I hope her big sister is a fan too."

This time Bess blushed. "Well—," she began to say, when Stacey shouted, "Austin, are you coming to breakfast or not?"

"Coming!" Austin called back. He shot Bess one last grin before hurrying to the table.

"Those pictures prove he's clean," I said as he left the dining room. "Though I still don't get why he's here every day."

"Because he's in love," George said matter-of-factly.

"Huh? What—with me?" Bess cried. "George, he might have a little crush on me, that's all."

"Austin's had a 'little crush' on you since the day of the Malachite meeting," George said.

"That's it!" I said. "Austin Gruber didn't volunteer to sabotage the party—he volunteered so he could be around Bess!"

"For your information," Bess said, jutting out her chin, "Austin is cute, but I don't have a crush on him. He's two years younger than me."

Then she rubbed her hands together. "Wait until I tell Maggie," she said. "She'll be totally psyched."

"Or totally jealous," George said.

I was relieved we had ruled out Austin, but that still left plenty of questions unanswered and the case unsolved.

"Let's go out to the beach," I said. "The Blue

Greenies are our only suspects at this point—maybe we'll find something outside."

But as we stepped out onto the beach, we found something better than clues—we found the Blue Greenies themselves on their bright blue sailboat, bobbing on the ocean waves.

"Good. I'm going to see what they say about the fire," I said.

The boat was just a few feet from shore when we reached the ocean. I could see Cassie and Nathan holding a banner made from a white sheet. Painted in blue was: BEACH PARTY MUST DIE!

"What's your problem with the beach party?" George called out to them. "It's to *save* the beach. That's what you want, isn't it?"

"It's not the whole party we're against," Cassie called back. "It's Miss Zaza."

Miss Zaza? The shoes! Hmm ... the Blue Greenies?

"What do you have against Miss Zaza?" I asked.

"Isn't it obvious?" Nathan shouted. "The incredible Miss Z wore a gown made of cooked lobsters to the Grammy Awards."

"It was an insult to all helpless crustaceans," Cassie yelled. "Now that Stacey woman wants her to perform at a party to help the beach and save its wildlife."

"If that isn't bad enough," Nathan called out, "the guy cooking for the party is Chef André Walters."

"So?" Bess asked.

Cassie swayed back and forth as the boat bounced on a big wave. "Chef Walters specializes in seafood," she shouted. "How could Stacey be so heartless?"

"Is that why you set fire to the mansion last night?" I shouted out. "So the party would be called off?"

"Fire?" Nathan yelled back.

I was about to ask again when a voice behind us screamed, "Out of the way! Out of the way!"

Two more Blue Greenies were charging down the beach. One knocked into my shoulder as they raced past us into the water.

"Mission accomplished!" cheered one of the runners, a guy wearing wraparound sunglasses, as he and his companion jumped into the boat. "Booyah!"

The motor roared as the boat sped off.

"Mission accomplished?" I asked as we watched the boat bounce away. "What did they mean by that?"

"Nancy, who cares?" George said. "It's pretty obvious the Blue Greenies are sabotaging this event, right?"

Not necessarily.

Ever since I was in third grade solving mysteries, my dad had told me to explore all options before declaring someone guilty, and that meant—

"We need more evidence," I blurted.

"Evidence?" George said.

"They hate Miss Zaza, Chef Walters—and McMansions," Bess asked. "How much more evidence do we need?"

Bess and George were right in a way. The evidence against the Blue Greenies was overwhelming—but something told me to keep this case open, even though I couldn't quite put my finger on what that something was.

"How would the Blue Greenies have gotten into the house to sabotage the shoes and set the fire?" I asked. "There's no way they could have a key. And there was no sign of breaking in."

For once, George didn't have a quick comeback. She finally said, "Okay, okay, we'll look for more clues."

Back inside the mansion we found not clues—but chaos!

"Ooh!" Austin groaned as he clutched his stomach. "I think I'm going to hurl."

Mandy's hand was clapped over her mouth. "I'll never eat seafood again," she said through her fingers. "Not even gummy fish."

All three Casabian sisters and Austin were doubled over. What had happened?

"I don't get it," Chef Walters cried. "I used only the freshest ingredients like I always do."

"As if!" Mia cried. "What are you trying to do, André—poison us?"

"Poison?" Bess gasped. "Is that what happened?"

Austin gagged. He stood up and ran out of the dining room to find a bathroom.

"Quick, Wayne," Bev shouted to the cameraman. "Get a close shot of the chef's face."

I stared at the platters of half-eaten seafood. The Blue Greenies had just admitted they despised Chef André Walters. Had that been their mission? To poison the party?

# POISED FOR POISON

**S**tacey was livid. "André," she fumed, "did you experiment with some new recipes?"

"Excuse me," Chef Walters said, narrowing his eyes. "Are you saying the bad food was my doing?"

"Don't put words in my mouth, André," Stacey said. "I only suggested that maybe—"

"Maybe you should get yourself a new chef for your party," André snapped. "Or order takeout."

The chef headed for the door.

"André, you can't quit days before the party," Stacey cried.

"Watch me!" he screamed.

Stacey's shoulders drooped as the chef marched out of the dining room. When she realized she was being filmed, she glared at Bev and shouted, "Okay, show's over. Get that camera out of our faces—now!"

I was happy to see the camera crew dart out of the dining room, but the feeling didn't last. We had a serious situation on our hands.

"My party—and my career—are imploding before my eyes," Stacey moaned. "When word gets out what's happening to this event, I'll never eat lunch in this town again."

"Do you have to mention *eat*?" Mallory groaned.

"Olgaaaaa!" Stacey shouted.

But Olga had been standing in the dining room all that time. She startled Stacey as she appeared right behind her.

"Olga, make the Casabian sisters some herbal tea," Stacey ordered. "I'll call my doctor and ask him what we should do."

"Sure," Olga murmured.

The housekeeper walked past, tossing her hair away from her face. How weird: This time her crooked nose looked *straight* again.

*Quit it, Nancy,* I thought. *There are more important things to focus on than Olga's nose.*

Like the tainted food.

"I hope the food wasn't poisoned," I whispered to Bess and George. "If it was, I have a pretty good idea who pulled it off."

"Blue Greenies," George answered. "Now do you believe those nuts are guilty as charged?"

"I suppose," I said. "Though I can't figure out how they could have gotten to the chef's food to poison it. One of his assistants in the kitchen would have seen them, for sure."

"They must have found some way," George said. "Guys, I really think it's time we talked to Stacey about everything we know."

The event planner was frantically texting as we walked over.

"Stacey, we think we know who tampered with the seafood," George said.

"You should also know what happened here in the middle of the night," Bess said. "Somebody—"

"Talk to me later," Stacey said. "I'm in crisis mode. I've got to find another performer *and* a chef." She hurried out of the dining room.

"We'll just have to try again later, when she's calmer," Bess said.

"Don't you mean *if* she's ever calmer?" I joked.

For the next hour or so the three of us sat with

Mandy, Mallory, and Mia as they sipped their tea. Austin's mom had already come to pick him up and take him to the doctor.

"I think I feel better now," Mallory said.

"Me too," Mia said. "That doctor Stacey called was right. It was probably a case of food poisoning."

"Literally," George added.

We suddenly heard Stacey's voice calling us from outside.

"Now what?" I said as we left the dining room.

When I looked outside, I gasped. Towering over Stacey in the driveway was a ginormous red creature— an inflated crab with huge claws and a sign around its neck that read LOVE ME, DON'T EAT ME!

"We're not even serving crab," Stacey cried. "Is the world going bonkers or what?"

We stared at the sign, written in bright blue letters. Hadn't we just seen another sign written in the same blue?

"The world's not going bonkers, Stacey," George said. "Just the Blue Greenics. We've been trying to tell you about this group."

"Who are they?" Stacey snapped. But before anyone could explain, she waved her hand and said, "I don't care. Just get rid of that thing before I slash it with my nail file."

Stacey had had just about enough. She walked through the gate and headed down the road to her beach house.

"Time to deflate Crabzilla," I said. Bess walked over to the balloon and unscrewed the cap on its claw. The three of us watched silently as the crustaceous balloon deflated.

"Nancy, who else *but* the Blue Greenies could be behind this massive sabotaging of the party? All signs point to them," Bess said.

"I know, I know," I said slowly. "But before we go to the police, I want to be *absolutely* sure."

"Then let's check out their blog," George suggested.

"The Blue Greenies have a blog?" I asked.

"Doesn't everybody?" George said. "The Blue Greenies use theirs to brag about their so-called successful missions. There's a computer in Inge's old office. Let's check it out."

Bess hesitated. "Can't we just use our phones to go online?"

"Relax, Bess. It'll be easier on a big screen, okay?" George said.

But once we filed into Inge's old office, we froze. Hanging on the wall behind her desk was Roland's portrait.

"George," I asked slowly, "didn't you take that thing down?"

"Definitely," she said, staring up at the portrait.

"So what's it doing back up there? Let's take it down and this time, out of the house," Bess said, reaching up to remove the painting.

"What *isn't* weird in this place?" George said. She went behind Inge's desk and sat down. Bess and I peered over her shoulders as she browsed the web for the Blue Greenies' blog.

The blog came up on the screen. The background was blue and had avatars of what looked like Cassie and Nathan carrying a smiling whale over their heads.

Underneath the avatars was a much more serious photo. It was of the oil-slicked bird that had been on our doorstep.

"Not only do they boast about their victories, they take pictures of them," I said.

George scrolled down to uncover another colorful shot. It was of the giant inflated crab outside the mansion. Underneath the picture was a caption that read: "We can't get inside the mansion, so poor Crabby has to stand outside."

"Wait a minute," I said, pointing to the monitor. "The Blue Greenies are admitting that they couldn't get inside the mansion."

"Maybe they were just talking about today," George

said. "They could have found a way to break in last night."

Farther down the page, beneath the picture of Crabzilla, were more shots of the Blue Greenies' escapades. One showed them attending a fancy seafood restaurant in Beverly Hills last night, where they freed live "imprisoned" lobsters from a tank.

"It says the lobsters were liberated by all the Blue Greenies at six p.m.," Bess said, reading the caption. "Just as the restaurant began serving dinner."

"Six p.m.," I repeated. "That's the time Miss Zaza was here to rehearse last night. They couldn't have been in the mansion sabotaging her shoes."

"Especially since they spent the entire night in a Beverly Hills stationhouse," George said. "They posted a shot of that, too."

I looked to see where George was pointing. On the screen was another shot of the Blue Greenies giving thumbs-ups in what looked like a holding cell. A clock on the cinder-block wall read three o'clock. Three a.m., no doubt.

"What time was the fire last night?" I asked.

"It was actually early in the morning," George said. "When I looked at the clock, it was around two thirty."

"So if the Blue Greenies spent all night at the stationhouse," I said, "that's their alibi for the time the fire was set."

"Come to think of it," Bess said, "if they did sabotage Miss Zaza's shoes and the chef's seafood, wouldn't they have bragged about it here on their blog?"

"You're right. Then that pretty much clears the Blue Greenies," I said. "Which means we're down to zero suspects."

But I wasn't about to quit. Not with the party a week away.

We took Roland's portrait with us as we headed toward the door, but just then I caught a whiff of something—kind of like a combo of chemicals and powder.

"Bess, are you wearing a new sunscreen?" I asked, knowing better than to ask George.

"No," Bess said. "Just my usual coconut."

I sniffed the air. "Definitely not coconut," I said, shaking my head.

By now Bess and George smelled it too. The three of us followed our noses to the door on the other side of the office. The smell was definitely stronger there.

"That's Roland's old office," I said. "Where we heard the bump the other day."

"Great," Bess groaned. "You think that smell is his dead body?"

George pulled at the doorknob. The door was locked, just as it had been the other day.

"Anybody in there?" George called, pounding on the door.

Nothing.

"I wish there was a way to get inside," I said.

"Who says we can't?" Bess said. She walked over to Inge's desk and picked up a letter opener. Then she used it to jimmy the lock.

I smiled as she pushed the door open just a crack. She may have been a fashionista, but when it came to fixing—and unfixing—things, she was a pro.

Bess pushed the door open. We didn't find anyone inside the office, but we did find the source of the strong smell.

"Look," I said, pointing to Roland's old desk. Scattered all over the top were pots, tubes, and compacts of makeup.

"Whoa," George said. "And I thought *you* had a lot of makeup, Bess."

"I certainly don't have any of these," Bess said as she lifted a case filled with fake fleshy noses, chins, and even mustaches.

Looking around, I found a Styrofoam wig head on the windowsill—without a wig.

"Where did this stuff come from?" I asked.

"Wait a minute," Bess said. "Didn't Stacey say that Inge was a Hollywood makeup artist? Maybe she used all this stuff when she was in Roland's cult."

It was possible, but when I examined the makeup brushes, I shook my head.

"These brushes are still wet," I pointed out. "Like they were recently used."

"By, maybe, Inge?" Bess asked with a gasp. "Nancy, what if the police didn't take Inge in? What if she—"

"You guys," George called from the other side of the office. "Check this out."

She was pointing to a large computer monitor standing on a table. On the screen was a grid of surveillance monitors—the kind lobby guards use to watch the floors of an office building.

"What do you think Roland used this for?" George asked.

Leaning forward, I took a closer look. I could see various rooms throughout the mansion.

"To watch his followers?" I said. "But the question is, who's using it now? And whose makeup is this? Is someone undercover?"

At that moment, my phone beeped. It was a text from Stacey, telling us she needed us ASAP.

"Stacey's back," I whispered. "Not a word about us sneaking into Roland's office."

We quietly left Roland's office, then Inge's. Stacey was in the living room, checking her ever-present phone.

"Delivery . . . two p.m.," Stacey read. She then

looked up at us and smiled. "There you are. Thanks for getting rid of that tacky crab."

"Do you need us to do anything else?" I asked.

"Yes!" Stacey said. "I need you to leave."

"Leave?" the three of us said in unison.

"Just for a few hours," Stacey explained. "Go to Universal Studios or Rodeo Drive. You're here for vacation, as I recall."

"But aren't there a million more things to do before the party? Why do you want us to leave?" I asked.

"I asked everyone in the house to clear out," Stacey said. "I have a *huge* surprise coming this afternoon and want it kept under wraps."

"What is it?" Bess asked.

"Honey, it wouldn't be a surprise if I told you," Stacey said. She gestured at the front door. "So go ahead and take the afternoon off. You worked hard, so you deserve it."

We really were reluctant to leave, but as I went to thank Stacey, I suddenly noticed a big red mark on her right arm. It didn't look like a birthmark, more like a burn.

"How'd you get that, Stacey?" I asked.

Stacey's brows flew up when she saw me looking at her arm. "Oh—I, um, burned myself at my last event. I reached over a tall pillar candle, and *ouch*. No big deal."

She opened the door and brushed us outside. "Have fun!" she called before tossing a pair of keys into George's hand. "Take my car keys. Can't get anywhere in L.A. without a car. Buh-bye!" She slammed the door shut. We turned and walked down the driveway, away from the mansion.

"You don't get a burn like that from a candle flame," George said.

"That's what I thought," I said.

Suddenly I felt someone behind us. At the car, I saw Olga coming down the driveway, carrying a bunch of plastic bags.

"Hi, Olga," George said, nodding at the bags in Olga's hands. "Trash day?"

Olga gave a little grunt, but as she walked by us, I thought I heard her mumble, "Garbage in, garbage out, all day long."

We froze.

Had she just said, *Garbage in, garbage out*?

# SECRET IDENTITY

**W**e gaped at Olga as she hurled white plastic bags onto the curb. *Garbage in, garbage out* was what Roland and his fanatical followers had chanted as they symbolically dumped trash into the ocean.

"Why did Olga just say Roland's mantra?" Bess asked.

I studied Olga's fake-looking hair, dark glasses, and bulbous nose, which had gone from looking crooked to straight. I remembered the case of fake noses we'd found in Roland's office and the makeup and Styrofoam wig head. Oh, no—could *Olga* possibly be *Inge*?

"I wonder what Olga looks like without her makeup," I told Bess and George.

"What do you mean?" George asked.

"Watch," I said.

I approached Olga, who had stopped to drink from a water bottle—with a Bubbling Brooks label, just like the bottle we'd found near Miss Zaza's shoes!

"Excuse me, Olga," I said. "Doesn't this garbage go in?"

"Garbage in?" Olga said. "No, garbage out . . ." and she looked me straight in the eye, dropped the water bottle, and ran.

But not before I grabbed a handful of her hair and yanked.

The wig flew off Olga's head. Underneath, blond hair was sticking out like a dandelion puff. The blond hair of Inge!

As Inge raced down the driveway, her sunglasses flew off and her fake nose started to wobble. Still running, she pulled the rubber nose off and threw it in our direction.

"Catch her!" I shouted. "Don't let her get away!"

We thundered down the road after Inge, who sped past Stacey's beach house.

"Stacey's car!" George said, pulling the keys from her pocket. "Get in."

The three of us jumped into the car. George gunned the engine and shot off after Inge.

Inge glanced over her shoulder. The car was just a few feet behind her when she switched direction, darting off the road into the brush.

"I can't drive off the road!" George cried.

"Then stop the car," I said.

George swerved over to the side of the road. We got out, then ran down the rocky, brushy hill after Inge.

"How am I supposed to run in sandals?" Bess complained as we practically skidded down the hill.

By now Inge had a good twenty feet on us. Just as I began picking up speed, I felt my footing give way. Pebbles and rocks flew as I slid down the steep, rocky hill.

I prayed not to slam into a tree. Instead I slammed right into Inge, knocking her off her feet and sending her rolling down the hill, screaming all the way.

"Omigod—where does that hill lead?" Bess asked. "What if she falls off a cliff?"

Suddenly we heard a loud *crunch*.

Inge had crashed feetfirst into a huge tree.

"Ouch," I said, wincing.

"That's got to hurt," George said.

Inge lay sprawled at the foot of the tree, writhing

in pain, as we scrambled down the hill. "My foot!" she shouted, trying to sit up. "I think it's broken."

"I'll call the police," Bess said, out of breath.

"Come on, Inge," George commanded. "Nancy and I will help you back up the hill."

As we slowly walked up the embankment, the hobbling Inge had her arms around our shoulders. It might not have been the ideal time to question her, but it probably would be the *only* time we had to find out the facts.

"What are you doing back here, Inge?" I demanded. "Aren't you supposed to be behind bars?"

Then George started in. "We know you're a master of disguise, Inge," she said. "But why did you move back into the mansion?"

"You couldn't have been thinking of reviving that dumb cult of Roland's, could you?" Bess asked.

Inge howled from the pain. She snapped, "*You* took care of our cult. It was my turn to take care of Stacey."

*Stacey?* "What does Stacey have to do with it?" I asked. "Don't tell me you're against the 'save the beach' party too."

"Party!" Inge scoffed so sharply it made me flinch. "Stacey is more than just a party planner. When Roland was alive, she was his biggest follower."

Bess gave a little gasp. "Nancy—the book in Stacey's desk, remember?"

Or course I did. Stacey seemed to know more about Roland and the mansion than we'd thought. I also remembered how I'd dismissed the idea of Stacey belonging to Roland's cult.

"That's crazy, Inge," I said. "Stacey hardly knew Roland."

"Oh, yes?" Inge said. "Why do you think she invited you girls to her house in Malachite in the first place?"

"She invited us because my mom worked with her years ago," George answered firmly. "It was her way of returning a favor."

Inge laughed. "That's rich! The only reason Stacey invited you was so you would eventually fall under Roland's spell. Roland loved new recruits, and Stacey would do anything for Roland."

"Stacey is a successful event planner," I said. "Why would she need somebody like him?"

"Two words," Inge said. "Money . . . and power."

"Define money and power," Bess said.

A dreamy look appeared on Inge's face as she explained. "Roland was a rising star. Sales of his book were up. More and more followers signed up for his program every week. In just a few years he would have a tremendous following and influence. Now, please let me sit for just a moment."

Bess said, "We'll rest near this rock for two minutes, but that's it."

Inge leaned against a huge rock. She looked awful.

"Stacey has plenty of her own money," I said. "She wouldn't have a beach house on Malachite if she didn't."

"You can never have enough money on Malachite Beach," Inge said. "If I may remind you, Stacey's house is a shack compared to the mega mansions around here."

Each time she mentioned Stacey's name, Inge seethed.

"If you and Stacey were both so devoted to Roland," I said, "why do you hate her so much?"

"Roland is dead," Inge said, blinking back tears. "If Stacey was so devoted to him, she'd be mourning his death, not celebrating it."

"Celebrating?" I asked.

"Isn't it obvious?" Inge said. "Stacey is using Roland's beloved mansion as a set for her ridiculous Hollywood party. Not only did she have the audacity to renovate it, but those *House Busters* clowns removed all traces of him."

"Thank goodness," Bess said softly.

"Stacey was destroying Roland's memory," Inge said firmly. "I had to find a way back into the mansion and stop the madness."

I stared at her. Stop the madness—or stop the party?

"So *you* sabotaged the party plans," I told Inge. "You poured water in Miss Zaza's shoes, set the fire in the middle of the night, and tampered with Chef Walters's food."

Inge didn't hesitate. She jutted her chin out and said, "I did, and if I had the chance, I'd do it again."

"Inge, you could have killed innocent people!" Bess said angrily. "Just like you could have killed us and so many others at your crazy cult."

"Killing *people* wasn't my plan," Inge said. "Killing that pathetic *party* of Stacey's was."

That explained why Inge had sabotaged the party, but it didn't explain something else. . . .

"You're supposed to be in prison, Inge," I said. "We saw the police arrest you the day of the explosion."

"You're right," Inge said with a sly smile. "They did take me in."

"Then how . . . ?" Bess started to say.

"Luckily, one of the prison guards was a Roland follower and helped me escape," Inge said. "I was also lucky that my old keys to the mansion still worked."

It wasn't long before the police and EMT workers showed up. Bess, George, and I watched as the queen of disguises was carried up the hill on a stretcher.

"I bet Inge was hiding out and sleeping in Roland's office," George said in disgust. "How pathetic."

"At least we found out who sabotaged Stacey's party," I said as we reached the car. "Looks like we solved another case, girls."

"But what about all that stuff Inge said about Stacey?" Bess asked. "Do you really believe she was part of Roland's cult?"

I shook my head and said, "I wouldn't believe anything that wacky woman told us, would you?"

"Yeah," George agreed. "Inge would have tried to pull the plug on that party no matter who was giving it."

We drove the short way to Stacey's beach house and parked the car in the driveway. By now even Bess was too exhausted to go to Rodeo Drive.

"Stacey's probably still working on her surprise, whatever it is," George said. "Let's hang out on her deck, then we'll go over and tell her we caught the sabotager."

"You mean *saboteur*," Bess corrected. "It's a French word."

*"Pardonne-moi!"* George said.

From the deck we could see Mia walking up the beach toward the house. The closer she got, the more upset she looked.

"What's wrong, Mia?" I asked as she climbed the steps to the deck. "Is something up?"

"I hope you and your sisters are feeling better," Bess said.

"We are." Mia nodded. "Mallory felt well enough to keep her appointment with Dr. Raymond today."

George grimaced and said, "You mean that plastic surgeon?"

"Did something go wrong at the doctor's?" I asked.

"No, no, no," Mia said, shaking her head. "Mallory's fine."

"Then what happened?" I asked.

"I went with Mallory, and she was just going to speak to the doctor about our contest. You know, where the winner gets the plastic surgery procedure of her choice?"

"Yeah, we know," George said.

"While Mallory was talking to Dr. Raymond, I went to get some water," Mia went on. "On the way down the hall, I passed the recovery room. I looked inside for a second and saw this man sitting in a chair facing the door. His face was totally covered with bandages except for his eyes."

"He probably had major work done," I said. "If that's what's upsetting you, I'm sure the doctor gave him meds for his pain."

"It's not that," Mia said. "His eyes were a piercing shade of light blue, and they were staring straight at me. The minute I saw those eyes, I knew whose they were."

"Whose?" I asked.

*"Roland's,"* Mia whispered, her voice cracking. "I could swear they were."

We all looked at Mia. She was wringing her hands and looked like she was about to cry.

"Mia, listen," I said gently. "I know you had a horrible experience in that cult. So did Bess and I, but Roland is dead."

Mia's shoulders dropped as she groaned under her breath. "Now you're telling me I'm imagining this," she said. "Look, I know what I saw, and I know that guy underneath those bandages was Roland!"

"Okay, okay," I said trying to calm her. "Did you ask anyone at the doctor's office who it was?"

"I was too scared to," Mia admitted. "I told Mallory after we left the office, but she thought I was crazy too."

"We don't think you're crazy, Mia," I said. "I just don't think Roland is still alive."

"Whatever," Mia grumbled, and then she stormed off the deck. When she was off our beach and out of earshot, I turned to Bess and George.

"She's still freaked out about the cult," I said. "No wonder she thinks she saw Roland."

"Unless he rose from the dead," George said with a laugh. "Or from the ashes of his burning yacht like a phoenix—"

"What if it's true?" Bess interrupted. "What if Mia really *did* see Roland? It's not like anybody ever found his body after the explosion, right?"

"Even Inge said Roland was dead, Bess," George said.

"She may *think* he's dead," Bess said. "Inge was hauled off to jail right after Roland's yacht blew up. How would she even know?"

Bess had a point. Though I didn't believe the bandaged man Mia had seen was Roland—even the idea freaked me out—we couldn't definitively rule it out.

"Okay then, let's go to Dr. Raymond's and see for ourselves," I said. "Stacey wanted us to disappear for a while anyway."

George heaved a sigh as she pulled out her phone. "I'll look up his address," she said. "What if we need an appointment?"

"An appointment could take weeks," Bess said.

"We don't need to see the doctor," I said. "I know it won't be easy, but we just have to get inside that recovery room and check out that bandaged man."

After browsing a few more seconds, George held up her phone. "Dr. Raymond's office is right on Rodeo Drive," she said before throwing Bess a warning look. "Don't even think of going shopping."

On our way to Rodeo Drive, we passed Roland's mansion. A black truck was now parked outside.

"I bet that's the flower delivery," Bess said.

"Too early for that," I said. "Maybe it has something to do with Stacey's surprise. Whatever that is."

Once we hit Rodeo Drive, I had to admit it was pretty awesome. Walking from the car to the doctor's office, I couldn't help gazing into the windows of the high-end stores and salons. George had a hard time dragging Bess away from the windows as she practically pressed her nose against the glass!

Just as impressive was Dr. Raymond's office, with its plush white carpet, exotic flower arrangements, and gold-framed mirrors.

We already had a plan when we stepped up to the reception desk. First, we would find a way to see Dr. Raymond. And once we were in the back, one of us would find a way to check out the recovery room.

"Hello," I said to the receptionist. "I'd like to see Dr. Raymond for a consultation."

The tanned receptionist, whose name plate read KENDRA, smiled up at me. "Certainly," she said. "Do you have an appointment?"

"No," I said.

"Oh, you need an appointment to see the doctor," Kendra replied. She glanced at her computer screen. "Dr. Raymond's earliest appointment is exactly . . . six months from today."

"Six months?" George cried.

"Nancy can't wait that long," Bess said. "This is an emergency."

"An emergency?" Kendra said, looking me up and down. "What's wrong with her?"

"Nancy is competing in a beauty pageant in three weeks," Bess blurted. "It's her first one, and just look at her! She needs all the help she can get."

I shot Bess a sideways glance. Couldn't she have come up with something better than that?

We waited for an answer. Kendra pursed her lips and said, "Sorry. I can call you if we have a cancellation."

George heaved a big sigh and said, "The Casabian sisters never have to wait this long. They told us getting an appointment with Dr. Raymond would be easy."

As we turned away from the desk, Kendra called, "Wait! You know Mandy, Mallory, and Mia?"

"We live next door to Villa Fabuloso," I said.

"Well, then," Kendra said, smiling back at her computer. "Let's see if I can squeeze you in today. I'm sure it won't be a problem." After a few seconds she looked up. "The doctor will see you in a few minutes," she said. "Why don't you make yourselves comfortable in the waiting room?"

The three of us sat side by side on the sofa.

"You and Bess can see Dr. Raymond," George

whispered. "I'll check out the recovery room and this bandaged guy."

"You don't know where the recovery room is," Bess whispered.

Just then a door near the reception desk marked MEDICAL TRANSCRIPTION opened. A woman walked out and said, "Kendra, I'm going to lunch. Want anything?"

"Just some of that vitamin water I like," she answered as the woman left the office. "Thanks, Shanna."

"Medical Transcription is where they keep the records," I whispered. "If Roland had work done here, I bet there are records, too."

"Bingo!" George whispered. "I want to sneak in there, but how can I get past Kendra?"

At that moment the receptionist looked up and said, "Nancy? The doctor will see you in his office now. You can bring your friends if you'd like."

The three of us stood up.

"Can you bring us to his office, please?" I asked. "We've never been here before."

"It's right over there." Kendra pointed down the hall.

"Nancy's a little nervous," Bess said. "It's her . . . first time."

"Oh, okay!" Kendra said, standing up. "Follow me."

I glanced over my shoulder at George. She was

already inching her way toward the Medical Transcription office.

*All systems go,* I thought.

Kendra opened the door to Dr. Raymond's office, and we stepped inside.

Dr. Raymond stood up from behind his desk. He looked more like a middle-aged movie star than a doctor.

"So who is Nancy?" he asked, grinning with perfectly straight teeth.

"I am," I said. "This is my friend Bess."

The doctor had Bess and me sit in chairs facing his desk. After he sat down again, he said, "I understand you're friends with the Casabian sisters, and that you're having a beauty crisis."

"I guess you could call it that," I said.

"If I may share my thoughts," Dr. Raymond said. He leaned over his desk to study my face. "Your nose is a bit fleshy, your left ear sticks out a bit, and your lips could use a little plumping."

"Excuse me?" I asked.

"And though you're still a teenager," the doctor went on, "I'd start some chemical peels as soon as possible. It's never too early to tackle sun damage."

He held up a mirror and said, "I'm also noticing frown lines."

"Um," Bess said. "Maybe because she's frowning?"

You bet I was frowning. This guy sounded more like Dr. Frankenstein!

"Can I think about what you said in the waiting room, doctor?" I asked. "I wouldn't want to make the wrong decision."

"Of course, Nancy, of course," Dr. Raymond said. "You know, we can schedule you for surgery perhaps as soon as next week if you'd like."

"Super!" I said, practically bolting out of the doctor's office.

Bess hurried down the hall after me. "I don't think your lips need plumping, Nancy," she said. "Lots of people have ears that stick out too."

"My ears don't stick out—and I happen to like my nose!" I said, lowering my voice to a whisper. "Now let's hope George is finished snooping."

When we reached the waiting room, I was happy to see George, pacing back and forth. Kendra was busy talking to another patient.

"Did anybody see you?" I whispered.

"No," George said. "Listen to what I found out. One of the files was for a Marty Malone."

"That's Roland's real name!" Bess gasped.

George nodded and went on. "Turns out Marty had plastic surgery the day of the yacht fire. He had the works—nose, eyes, face, even his hairline was changed."

I felt my blood turn to ice.

"According to the file, the surgery was scheduled for two thirty p.m.," George explained. "The surgery ended at exactly five p.m., which was when Marty— or Roland—went into recovery."

I tried to remember what time the yacht blew up. It was shortly after we had gotten back from the hospital that day.

"Roland's yacht blew up at around five thirty in the afternoon," I said. "If he was recovering from surgery, how could he have been on that yacht?"

"Especially after going under the knife and anesthesia," George said.

The three of us stared at one another, speechless. Finally Bess said, "Mia was right. The bandaged guy she saw today *was* Roland!"

# SINISTER SURPRISE

The thought of Roland still alive tied my stomach into tight little knots, but I still had to see him with my own eyes.

"We have to find the recovery room and see for ourselves," I said in a low voice.

"I don't want to see Roland again," Bess said. "Who knows what he's capable of—remember, he's crazy."

"After surgery and stitches?" George said. "He'll be lucky if he can open his mouth."

Kendra was busy paying Shanna for the vitamin water, so we slipped past her desk and down the hall. This time we walked past Dr. Raymond's office, glancing into each room—a kitchen; the supply room; another, smaller waiting room. A woman wearing pink scrubs walked by but was too busy reading a patient's chart to notice us.

Suddenly I caught a whiff of alcohol. I looked to an open door at the end of the hallway. Through it I saw two hospital beds—one empty and one occupied by a person whose head was covered with bandages.

"There's the recovery room, but is that Roland?" George whispered.

"There's only one way to find out," I said.

We slipped into the room, quietly approaching the bed. We looked at the person wrapped in bandages. But what we saw wasn't Roland. It was a teenage girl.

The girl's eyes popped open. "Hi," she said drowsily. "How do I look?"

"Can I help you?" A voice made me jump.

We spun around to see the woman in pink scrubs walking through the door. I guessed from the blood pressure monitor she was wheeling in that she was a nurse.

"Hi," I said with a smile. "We were just touring your facilities—for when I have surgery."

"You'll definitely be in good hands," the nurse said as she parked the monitor next to the bed. "Just like Emily here."

The girl tried to sit up. "Does anyone have a mirror?" she mumbled. "I want to see what I look like."

"Not yet, honey," the nurse said. While she wrapped the BP band around Emily's arm, I studied the room. There was a curtained-off area. Was Roland behind that? There was also a closed door marked BATHROOM. Was Roland in there?

"Excuse me," I said to the nurse. "Someone we know just had surgery here, and we want to say hi. His name is Roland—I mean, Marty Malone."

"Mr. Malone just checked out today," the nurse replied.

"Checked out?" George said. "That wasn't in his file."

"She means that wasn't what Dr. Raymond had told us," I lied quickly.

"Mr. Malone checked out in a hurry," the nurse said. "Dr. Raymond might not have been informed yet."

"A hurry?" I repeated. Could Roland have bolted after realizing that Mia had seen him?

"This patient really needs her rest," the nurse told us. "Please go now."

We left the recovery room and headed back to the main waiting room.

"So, the eyes Mia saw *were* the eyes of Roland," I said.

"Then if Roland is alive," Bess said, "who blew up that yacht? Could he have pulled that off?"

"Whoever did it must have gotten injured—or burned," George said.

*Burned?* The burn on Stacey's arm!

"You guys," I said slowly. "Remember the burn on Stacey's arm? Do you think she got it from blowing up Roland's yacht?"

"And lived?" George cried.

"This may sound weird," I said. "But I have to check out the wet suit in Stacey's shed again. This time more closely. Don't forget, it *was* damp."

We left Dr. Raymond's office and drove back to Stacey's beach house. The wet suit was exactly where we had seen it the last time, hanging from a hook inside the shed.

I pulled the black suit off the hook and examined it from head to toe. Nothing.

I took it outside into the light and looked at it again. And there, on the right arm, was an oval-shaped hole about three inches long.

"Stacey's burn was right around this spot," I said.

"What makes you think it's a burn?" Bess asked. "Stacey could have ripped her sleeve."

"Coral can be pretty sharp," George added.

"The edges aren't ragged like in a rip," I pointed out. "They're charred like they were singed."

"I don't buy it," George said. "The yacht explosion was massive. No way anyone could have survived it."

"Unless she swam away from the yacht *before* it blew," I said.

"If Stacey planned to blow up the yacht," Bess said, "she would have to have known about those flammable oil drums."

"It doesn't add up, you guys," George said, shaking her head. "Why would Stacey want to ruin her own beach? You heard what she said—the oil spill drove her property value down."

"The only person who can answer that question is Stacey," I said, hanging the suit on the hook. "Let's go next door and find her."

We left the shed and walked to Roland's mansion. The black truck was gone. The house seemed eerily quiet.

"Stacey?" I called as we walked through the house. No answer.

"You think she knows we're onto something?" Bess asked.

"How would she?" George said. She turned toward the west wing. "Let's just split up and look for her. She could be anywhere in this place. Just holler—or text—if you see anything."

On the way to the west wing, we passed a door leading to the newly refurbished indoor pool. We still hadn't seen the pool, but I could smell chlorine through the half-opened door.

"I'll check to see if Stacey's down there and catch up with you guys," I called to Bess and George.

I opened the door. The smell of chlorine became stronger as I reached the bottom of the stairs and the pool area.

"Nice," I told myself as I gazed around.

Brand-new lounge chairs and white ceramic tiles surrounded an oval-shaped swimming pool. From where I stood, I saw no one swimming. The pool and the pool area were empty.

I was about to turn toward the door when a flash of silver on one of the lounge chairs caught my eye: Stacey's phone.

*Stacey's going to miss this,* I thought, picking it up. *She enters every second of her schedule in here.*

That's when I had a thought. If Stacey entered every detail in her phone, what had she written the day of the yacht explosion?

I scrolled down Stacey's jam-packed calendar until I reached the day of the explosion. The first thing I read was, DRIVE VEGAS 2 LA.

"Drive from Vegas to L.A.," I interpreted.

Something didn't click. According to this schedule, Stacey had driven home to L.A. the day of the explosion, *not* the morning after like she'd told us.

I looked to see what else Stacey had planned that day: 1:30 LUNCH W/DENISE; 3:00 LEAVE MSG WITH GRLS.

"Leave message with girls," I repeated softly. That was probably the message Stacey left saying she would be coming into L.A. the next day . . . when she was *already* in town.

I read on: 3:30 COFFEE & VITAMINS; 4:00 DRIVE 2 BCH HOUSE; 4:30 DIVING SUIT & SWIM 2 SITE; 5:00 BUY; 7:00 DIN W/BARB @ THE BLUE PALM.

Stacey had put on the wet suit that day. She'd also swum underwater to the "site," which was probably the yacht, but what did BUY mean?

Had Stacey bought something? Unless . . . BUY was an abbreviation or code for something, but what?

BUY . . . BUY . . . what? Flowers for the party? A new dress? It didn't make sense. *B* is for boy, blue, blow? I tried to guess.

"*Y* . . . is for yoga, yellow, yardstick, yacht—"
*Yacht!*

"BUY—Boy Yacht? Blue Yacht? Blow Yacht?"
Then I gasped. *Blow Up Yacht.*

My heart pounded inside my chest. There it was in Stacey's own words. She had blown up Roland's yacht, then had dinner with a friend at a well-known restaurant as if it was no big deal!

I had to show Stacey's phone to Bess and George

right away, but as I turned toward the door—

"I was just looking for that," Stacey said.

Clutching the phone, I spun around. Stacey was entering the pool area, her mouth a grim line.

"Come on," she said, holding out her hand. "Pony it up."

I gripped the phone tighter as I took a step back. No way would I give up the only evidence I had on the yacht explosion.

"Oh, puh-leeze," Stacey groaned. "Aren't you a little old to be playing finders-keepers?"

"I'm not the one playing games, Stacey," I said, nodding at her arm. "That burn isn't from a catering accident, and you know it. It's from blowing up Roland's yacht.

"Why'd you do it?" I continued. "You must have known about the flammable oil drums on the yacht. Why would you want to ruin your own beach?"

"Give me a break!" she said. "Would I be planning this whole 'save the beach' shindig if I wanted to pollute it?"

Stacey lunged for her phone. I stepped back until I was caught between two lounge chairs, my back to the pool. She came toward me, and I had nowhere to go but up on the diving board.

"Give me my phone," Stacey snapped, hopping up

on the diving board. She stood at the other end, her feet planted firmly on the board.

I didn't look down at the water for fear of becoming dizzy. I wasn't worried about falling into the pool, since I was a good swimmer, but I was worried about what Stacey would do to me.

"Mrs. Fayne told me you girls were detectives," Stacey said as she finally stopped inching forward. "Or maybe you're just playing detective to feel grown-up."

"Why don't *you* grow up, Stacey, and come clean?" I said. "It can all end right now."

"For me or for you?" Stacey smiled slyly. She then nodded at the water. "Why don't you say hello to my little friend?"

Friend? I gazed deep down into the pool and froze. Swimming at the bottom were two of the sea creatures Stacey had promised for the party. Not turtles or tropical fish, but *sharks!*

# DIVA OF DECEPTION

My knees buckled with fear. So that's what the black truck was delivering. How did Stacey ever pull that off?

The sharks weren't big, but I was sure their teeth were—and with Stacey perched at the other end of the diving board, I had nowhere to go but down.

"You can keep my phone or your life," Stacey said rather coolly. "All it would take is one tiny little push."

I looked her straight in the eye.

"You can try to get rid of me, Stacey," I said. "But I'm not the only one who knows your secret."

Stacey heaved a big sigh as she threw her arms in

the air. "I don't know why you keep insisting I would blow up a perfectly elegant yacht," she said. "What an unfortunate waste that would be."

One shark splashed in the water, and I cringed.

"Step back and get out of my way, Stacey," I said, holding her phone over the water. But then I had a brilliant idea: I'd dial 911!

"I'm calling the police!"

"Don't you dare. You can't prove a thing." Stacey's voice was calmer now. She made her way up the diving board toward me, her face filled with quiet rage.

If I took my eyes off her to look at the phone, she could rush at me. What should I do? Knock Stacey off the diving board first? Wrestle her? Or hit her where she was most vulnerable: her ego?

"You're right," I said, trying to sound nonchalant. "You'd have no good reason to blow up Roland's yacht. My guess is that it was really Inge Svenson."

Stacey snorted at the sound of Inge's name. "Inge?" she said. "What about Inge?"

"Inge is telling everyone *she* blew up Roland's yacht and polluted the beach," I said. "The press is having a field day—everyone wants an interview with Roland's number one partner in crime."

"The media?" Stacey gasped.

"Can you imagine the money she'll make from

interviews alone?" I went on. "Then there'll be book deals . . . movie rights . . ."

"Movie rights?" Stacey said under her breath. She narrowed her eyes. "Give me a break. That ridiculous woman couldn't blow up a balloon, let alone a yacht."

"You're right," I said, trying to remain calm. "You'd have to be a total genius to commit a crime like that and get away with it. I can't imagine who it could be."

"You're looking at her," Stacey blurted.

"Excuse me?" I said, inwardly excited. Was Stacey about to confess?

"Of course it wasn't my idea alone," Stacey said as she backed up on the diving board. "Roland and I hatched the plan after Leonard Stamp announced he'd be tearing down Roland's Renewal Retreat and Spa."

"Leonard Stamp, the real-estate tycoon?" I asked.

Stacey nodded and went on, "Since the mansion was a rental, Roland had no claim to it. There was no way he'd be able to make money. Leonard also had his snarky eye on my beach house. The two of us had to do something to save our homes."

I stepped forward ever so slightly.

"What did you do?" I asked.

"What else could we do?" Stacey said. "If we were going to stop Leonard, we had to bring our property values down. A messy oil spill would be perfect. After all, Malachite is all about its beaches."

Stacey lingered casually at the other end of the diving board, no longer guarding it like a pit bull.

"It wasn't easy," she continued. "But we managed to load those drums of flammable oil on his yacht without anyone knowing."

"Not even Inge?" I asked, inching forward.

"Especially not Inge," Stacey snapped. "I made sure of that."

"Go on," I said, trying to keep her calm. "How did you pull it off?"

"Roland and I were going to set off the explosion together," she explained. "My phone was programmed to blow up the yacht when the time was right."

"Your phone?" I gulped, glancing down at the phone in my hand.

"Oh, don't worry, it never worked," Stacey scoffed. "That's why I had to swim over to the yacht in that wet suit and set off the timer manually."

She glanced down at her burnt arm and said, "Unfortunately, I didn't swim far enough away from the burning yacht."

"Didn't you know Roland was on the run?" I asked. "Why would you want to do it alone?"

"Of course I knew Roland was on the run. I was the only person he told," Stacey said. "But I still wasn't going to let Leonard tear down my beach house, so I took matters into my own hands."

From the corner of my eye I could see the sharks darting back and forth under the water. The movement made me sway from side to side, but quickly I recovered my balance.

"I don't get it," I said. "If you wanted to destroy the beach, why are you planning this event to *save* it?"

"The money, honey!" Stacey declared. "I may be a Roland devotee, but I'm still one of Hollywood's most successful event planners. This event promises to make me even bigger—so who cares if Leonard Stamp tears down my house to build a McMansion? I'll just *buy* it!"

Stacey Manning was definitely a sick puppy, but if I was going to get off that diving board, I would have to keep talking.

"I guess I was wrong," I said, almost at the end of the diving board. "You really did have the brains to pull it off."

"Thanks, but my job isn't finished yet," Stacey said. I gasped as she hopped back onto the diving board. "There's just one little annoying matter I have to take care of first."

She moved slowly forward. I glanced down and saw the sharks circling underneath the diving board. There was only one way out. I'd have to knock Stacey off the board before she got to me.

I gritted my teeth and thrust out my arms, but before I could lunge at her—

"Don't move!" a deep voice shouted.

Stacey stopped in her tracks. Looking past her, I saw two Malachite Beach police officers, along with Bess and George, filing through the door.

"We saw you on the monitors in Roland's old office," George said. "We called the police immediately."

"Officers Kent and Rizzo came right away," Bess said with a smile.

"Whoa!" Officer Kent said, glancing into the water. "She sure did need help. There are sharks in this pool!"

Stacey looked almost bored as she hopped off the diving board onto the floor. I climbed off too, hurrying over to Bess and George.

"Is there a problem, officers?" Stacey asked coolly.

"Don't act coy," Officer Rizzo said. "And don't tell me you didn't know it was illegal to harbor live sharks in your swimming pool."

"Sharks?" Stacey said, pretending to gasp. "Well, once these girls started snooping, I changed my order from a harmless bottle-nosed dolphin to something, shall I say, a little more threatening."

While Officer Rizzo read Stacey her rights and snapped the cuffs on, I handed Officer Kent her phone.

"You might want to check this out, Officer," I said. "Stacey admitted to the yacht explosion and polluting the—"

"Blah, blah, blah," Stacey interrupted. "I'll be

happy to tell you everything, officers. And if there are cameras outside . . ."

While Officer Rizzo radioed the Malachite Beach stationhouse, Officer Kent led Stacey up the stairs. I was happy to see her go but had one last question. . . .

"Wait, Stacey," I called out. "If Roland wasn't on the yacht and he never killed himself, where is he?"

Stacey smiled broadly over her shoulder. "Roland never told me where he was going. I wouldn't worry if I were you. Knowing Roland—or Marty—he'll resurface somewhere, someday. You can be sure of that."

"All right, let's go," Officer Kent said.

I hugged my friends for coming to the rescue.

"Thanks, you guys," I said. "Swimming with sharks was definitely not on my vacation itinerary."

"Hey, what are friends for?" Bess said with a grin.

"I guess Stacey *did* blow up Roland's yacht," George said, shaking her head. "I still can't believe it."

"Believe it," I said. "Not only did she blow up the yacht, she's proud of it."

"To think she was raising money for a disaster she caused herself." Bess sighed. "Well, there goes that great party."

I planted my hands on my hips. "Hey, wait a minute, you guys," I said. "Why *can't* we still have a party to save Malachite Beach?"

"Nancy," George said. "Without an event planner—

even a maniacal one—how would we pull a party of this size off? There's the food, the entertainment, transportation, RSVPs—"

"We can't take care of all that on our own," Bess cut in.

"Who says we have to? I happen to know a super event planner in River Heights who probably would love a trip to sunny Malachite Beach," I said.

George's eyes lit up. "You mean my mom? Cool."

"And," I continued, "we know a twelve-year-old live wire named Alice Bothwell who I'm sure would love to help out."

"*And* a cute singer who'd love to perform at the party," Bess added.

"Austin Gruber!" George and I chorused.

The three of us exchanged our famous high five.

"Then after the party it's back to River Heights," Bess said with another sigh. "Even if it does mean cutting our vacation a few days short."

"Fine with me," George said. "After what we've been through, it'll be great to get back to normal."

Normal?

I knew I'd be ready to go home after the party too, but something inside me said things wouldn't be quite that normal—at least not right away.

"You heard what Stacey told us," I said. "Marty Malone—or Roland—is out there somewhere, and as long as he is, this mystery is *far* from over."

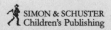